Matthew H. Jamison

Fort Leavenworth and the Soldiers' Home

Matthew H. Jamison

Fort Leavenworth and the Soldiers' Home

ISBN/EAN: 9783337308346

Printed in Europe, USA, Canada, Australia, Japan

Cover: Foto ©Andreas Hilbeck / pixelio.de

More available books at **www.hansebooks.com**

FORT LEAVENWORTH

AND THE

SOLDIERS' HOME

WITH SKETCHES OF

LEAVENWORTH

AND OF THE

MEN AND TRAGEDIES

THAT HAVE MADE HER FAMOUS.

INVALUABLE TO VISITORS, OF WHOM THERE ARE THOUSANDS
ANNUALLY.

PROFUSELY ILLUSTRATED.

COPYRIGHT 1906 BY

MATTHEW H. JAMISON,

WESTERN BRANCH NATIONAL HOME, D. V. S.
LEAVENWORTH COUNTY, KAS.

KANSAS CITY, MO.
H. & N. KIMBERLY PRINTING CO. PRINTERS AND BINDERS
1906

Anheuser-Busch Brewing Ass'n.
St. Louis, Missouri.
Brewers of FINE BEER Exclusively.

Our Brands:
Anheuser-Busch,
Standard,
The Original
Budweiser,
The Faust,
The Munchener,
The
Premium Pale,
The Exquisite.

Largest
Brewing
Capacity
of any Brewery
in the World,
2,000,000
Barrels and
100,000,000
Bottles
a Year.

WHITE LABEL
EXQUISITE

Our Motto in Buying Brew Materials is:
"NOT HOW CHEAP, BUT HOW GOOD."

8

PREFATORY.

To the old soldier, upon whom the world looks askance, who was a convenient refuge in the time of trouble, but who survives only in the derisive smile of Crœsus who lays his hand convulsively over his bags of gold at sight of the apparition of 1861, apprehensive of alms or plunder or both.

To the old soldier, shadow or relict of the Revolution, the granther of 1812, the volunteer on the plains of Mexico, the veteran under Grant the old soldier, him in the ranks, the integer in the stout column of one hundred thousand men, black with the grime of the pine-kno camp fires, his nostrils full of dust, his feet full of blisters, his havert sack full of sweet potatoes, his canteen full of wh——, his reast fu of loving kindness; whose eyes flash at the sound of the first gun lik glow-worm in the dark; who has a thousand miles in his wake and an other thousand before him, the poor lad, my comrade, from the fall of Sumter down to the last gasp of the dead and damned Confederacy ; who left his bones in the South as a pledge of his love for you and me—to his memory I dedicate these pages.

I bless God chiefly for this, that I have believed in something

In my youth I stood on Bunker Hill and worshiped on the spot where Warren fell, and in those early days of awakening and unquestioning faith, I looked up into the benignant face of Abraham Lincoln- and in those deeply graven, sad, and tragic lines read those lessons of sincerity, patience, and magnanimity unequaled in all the weary ages, and which will endure the glorious heritage of the youth of this dear land of ours.

Through him I came to know the full value of our American Union, that object-lesson in self-government, uplifted to aspiring races, around which is gathered an impregnable bulwark of defense; the most virile people on the globe—a nation of fresh young blood, augmented, renewed, and aërated by a continuous influx of the most adventurous and daring from the uttermost corners of the earth.

I believe, I wish to believe, and I do believe, that this mighty political fabric called the Federal Union is the head of column of the hosts of millennial civilization, that at two in the morning, when the morrow is as yet unlimned in the east, our cavalry advance is already in the saddle, feeling our way to that glad day, which, under God is ours by right of conquest.

MATTHEW H JAMISON,
Western Branch National Home D V. S., April, 1895.

The Greatest Retail House

IN THE WEST.

105 DEPARTMENTS.   STOCK, $1,250,000.
FLOOR AREA, NEARLY 7 ACRES.

Dry Goods, Millinery, Ladies' Suits,
Notions, Boys' Clothing, Men's Furnishings,
Shoes, Jewelry, Silverware, Books, Furniture,
Carpets, Wall Paper, Hardware, Candies, New Tea Room, etc.

Emery, Bird, Thayer & Co.,

SUCCESSORS TO

Bullene, Moore, Emery & Co.

Kansas City, Mo.

Swift and Company,

PORK PACKERS
and SHIPPERS of

DRESSED BEEF, PORK and MUTTON.

Kansas City.   Chicago.   South Omaha.   East St. Louis.

Premium Brand

Hams,
Breakfast Bacon and
Kettle-Rendered Leaf Lard.

A GLANCE AT

The Romantic History

OF THE

IMPERIAL DOMAIN KNOWN AS THE "LOUISIANA PURCHASE.

- ● ● -

Man is a nomad. Since the gates of Paradise closed behind him
he has been a globe trotter, always going somewhere and never getting
there, hustling to gather filthy lucre on the wing. The mystery of
something just beyond lured him on. He had compassed all lands,
and it would be hard to name a time when our so-called western wilds
were unknown to the adventurous footsteps of the questioning
Caucasian.

Lieutenant Pike penetrated the Southwest in 1806, and found
James Purcell at Santa Fé, who was there when Purcell arrived I know
not, but that there was a Yankee on top of one of those mountains,
sitting on a herring-box, whittling, no accepted historian could question
We know now that Columbus was a laggard discoverer, that Leif
Ericsson preceded him on the Atlantic coast by a thousand years or so,
and it is quite probable that the hardy mariners of northern Europe
had landed on these shores before the Christian era

The Mandan tribe of Indians in the Northwest, now almost extinct
but numbering twenty five hundred people at the beginning of the
century, are of Welch origin, and when discovered and in their purest
strain, had yellow hair, and some of them, the women in particular
beautiful white complexions. The shipwrecked or adventurous origin
of this small tribe is lost in obscurity, and can only be traced in their
language, but it doubtless extends back many centuries.

We know withal that Cabeza, following in the wake of Columbus
traversed our continent in 1534, and that the Spanish cavaliers under
Coronado in 1540 were the first white men, in military force to view
the plains of Kansas.

French exploring expeditions penetrated these regions early in the eighteenth century, and a Spanish expedition from Santa Fé, to counter the French attempt to take possession of the country, advanced to a point on the Missouri River just below the site of Fort Leavenworth, probably on the ground where the city of Leavenworth now stands, or on the grounds of the National Home, and here, at night, were .attacked by two thousand Indian braves and massacred to a man, excepting a priest, who escaped on horseback and returned to New Mexico. The Indians, stolid and indifferent, never could be persuaded to give up the details of this tragedy; which for mystery and diabolism stood for a century the prophecy of the shameless atrocities which stained the later history of Leavenworth County under the pale-face.

Just a century later, to-wit, in 1819, the first steamboat, named the *Western Engineer*, Major Stephen H. Long, commanding, passed up the Missouri River. Major Long, with a corps of topographical engineers, made a tour of observation aboard this craft, as far as the mouth of the Yellowstone. The boat was a sort of stern-wheel water-devil, built to lash the water with her tail and to vomit steam and smoke through her escape-pipe, which protruded at the prow in the shape of the head of an immense serpent with a red, forked tongue! The superstitious red man gave it a wide berth, under the impression that it was a "maniteau" which had come to destroy them.

Thomas Jefferson negotiated the purchase of this territory of unlimited and undefined boundaries from Buonaparte, First Consul of France, in 1803, for $16,000,000, of which amount $4,000,000 reverted to American claimants for French spoliations. "Boney" was hard up for the "sinews of war," and the sagacious Jefferson was as smooth as old Shylock himself in dealing with him, and this master-stroke—the Louisiana Purchase—has never ceased to be the wonder and admiration of both European and American statesmen; especially has it been the envy of and a thorn to the British. These international pirates and freebooters would wrest this vast domain away from us by the sword, and it was left to "Old Hickory" to receive them at New Orleans, and give their general, Packingham, a hospitable grave.

The far-seeing Jefferson placed a just estimate upon the vast empire that he had acquired west of the Mississippi for a mere song, and the year following, 1804, sent out the Lewis and Clark Exploring Expedition to its utmost boundaries.

It is worth while to remark, *en passant*, that the silver and gold output of this region for one year is worth double the purchase price. The wheat crop of any one of these Western States—Kansas or California—would pay the bill. Yea, it is only necessary for the women of this western empire to turn on the feed and their hens can take up a little obligation like that in one day. You can see for yourself that when "Boney" left the effete monarchies of Europe to monkey with a Yankee, that he wasn't in it; but let us shut up,—France got back on us when her Rothschilds made us a four per cent loan worth only two! That's what we get for plunging twice into the innocuous desuetude of Clevelandism. We will know better than to renew a disagreeable acquaintance next time—maybe! Internal earthquakes! when I think of that loan—but the Democrats always did think that we had "money to burn."

I see: our muttons are getting cold, and we will resume. Lieutenant Pike, as already hinted, under orders from the Government, led an expedition as far as the Rocky Mountains in 1805, and christened the lofty peak which bears his name. And enterprising trappers, hardy and daring men, friendly with the Indians, and who became identified with the tribes by marriage, pitched their camps among the haunts of the beaver in the most remote and inaccessible wilds. Here we find Kit Carson and old Bill Williams, who gave Carson his first lesson in frontier life, as early as 1820 and before, when for twenty years they never slept under a roof nor saw the face of a white woman. When we reflect upon the privations and perils endured by these early explorers, trappers, and hunters, many of whom are not mentioned in these pages, but who were as familiar with our western country to its most distant verge as the reader is with his own back yard, it seems incredible that the public ever could have been carried away by so transparent a fraud as the alleged explorations of John C. Frémont, who, two hundred years after Cabeza and Coronado, fifty years after the trappers and forty years after Lewis and Clark, scaled a mountain and unfurled the flag of his country as an original explorer.

After "Uncle Tom" Benton had become reconciled to the young lieutenant who had run away with his daughter, he stood up in his place in the Senate, and in picturesque solemnity gave a soul-harrowing picture of the skeleton men of Frémont's picnic excursion leading skeleton horses over trackless wastes of snow in regions which his guide, Kit Carson, and his companion-trappers had traversed, back and forth, twenty times without thought of being considered heroes

Encouraged by the eloquence of his father-in-law, the "Pathfinder" tumbled to his role and made the most of it; gravely announcing to a dazzled universe that "having been where human foot never trod before, we felt the exaltation of first explorers!" Shades of innocent old Pickwick! Sage, serious, heroic Pickwick! bestir thyself; here's another rival! Kit found the trail for him and directed the course of the journey, but the "Pathfinder's" admiring biographer, thrilled with the enthusiasm of campaign eulogy, proceeds to congratulate the country on his hero's "*safe return to the United States*"! Frémont was useful in a small way, in the sense that he represented the sovereignty of the Government over the Pacific coast country through which he passed, carrying the standard of the Republic as against the threatened encroachments of Great Britain.

The record of this "original explorer" is further relieved, according to his own veracious pen, by a charge which he made in his own valorous person upon a herd of retreating buffaloes. He was not dismayed, he tells us, but while Carson stopped to skin one of the beasts which he had slain, the "Pathfinder" plunged fearlessly on and brought down a bull with his revolver; exploiting himself with better effect in this affair than he displayed when old Colonel Mason called him down! Nor can one restrain the feeling that our doughty explorer should have nursed his courage for later contingencies under "Pap" Price, or as a bracer against his propensity to turn tail before Stonewall Jackson "in the valley."

How narrowly John C. Frémont escaped having greatness thrust upon him! In 1856 the popular vote for President of the United States was obsequiously laid at his feet. And for what? Riding with a handful of men through to California in the wake of Kit Carson, and for twice repeating the performance!

In youth my admiring fancy lightly divided—oscillated in painful uncertainty—between Phineas T. Barnum, the apocryphal Woolly Horse, and the "Pathfinder," and I am still in vague, three-cornered doubt as to which of these is most entitled to posthumous honors.

Having given our attention in the foregoing introductory lines to a hasty survey of the vast domain in which we are situated, let us come at once to the point.

Fort Leavenworth, the city of Leavenworth, and Leavenworth County comprise a triumvirate famous in the annals of Kansas, and in the history of the Republic. But our interest for the present lies

ESTABLISHED 1873

D. P. Thomson

PHOTOGRAPHER, 1000-1002 WALNUT STREET, KANSAS CITY, - MISSOURI.

briefly in the following, to-wit: The Fort, the city, the N_____ed H__me,
and the K_____ State Prison which lie in echelon along the we__
___ ___ the Miss___ Ri___ the order n____. They c____ in.
_ ___ the ___ ___ ___ t that the St__ Pr__ _
N__ H____ ___ ___ miss__n.

___ ___ ___ ___ ___ ___ ___ ___
___ ___ ___ ___ ___ ___
___ ___ ___ ___ ___ ___ ___
___ ___ ___ ___ ___ ___ ___
___ ___ ___ ___ ___ ___ ___
___ ___ ___ ___ ___ ___ ___
___ ___ ___ ___ ___ ___ ___
___ ___ ___ ___ ___ ___
___ ___ ___ ___ ___ ___
___ ___ ___ ___ ___ ___

plex perspective the divinity which hedges us about, which thwarts our purpose, which, when we would go here, with commanding finger says, "Go there!" and we go, whether we will or no.

Under orders from the War Department, Col. Henry H. Leavenworth, 3d U. S. Infantry, with four companies of his regiment, proceeded to select the site for "a permanent cantonment, on the left bank of the Missouri River, within twenty miles of the mouth of the Little Platte, above or below that point." In pursuance of these instructions, Col. Leavenworth directly violated them by fixing the site on the right or Kansas shore instead of the left or Missouri bank, for the very good reason that no suitable ground could be found on the latter.

With delightful confidence in his own infallibility and discretion, early in June, 1827, before the official approval of his selection reached him, the erection of log barracks was begun and the post named "Cantonment Leavenworth," a name retained down to the year 1832, when it became "Fort Leavenworth," under orders from the War Department changing the names of all "Cantonments" to "Forts."

The reservation contains nine square miles, or 7,000 acres. The original Fort composed a square, on each of the four corners of which was a log block-house, pierced for musketry. Within this square were the officers' quarters, the warehouses, and stables. This structure gave way in time to more permanent improvements, and there is still standing, on a line with the south end of McPherson Hall, extending eastward, a heavy stone wall, pierced for musketry, and with an embrasure for one gun, the whole being a relic of the earliest provision against attack by Indians or other foes. The original four companies brought with them into the wilderness four cows, which, together with their calves, were corralled on rising ground in rear of the camp, which as yet was unprovided with defences, and one night the soldiers were aroused by a great bellowing and commotion in the cattle-yard. A prowling bruin had scented meat from the neighboring jungle, followed up the wind, and attacked the calves, which brought the maternal bovines with a rush to the rescue, and four to one proving too much for the bear, he made a break for the brush, taking a course in his precipitate flight directly toward the company tents, one of which he dashed through, bringing down poles and tent in the general wreck, the boys yelling, some firing at the brute, which scorned all opposition and in the most nimble and enterprising fashion cleared out with a whole hide.

History, let us remind the reader, ought to be written with due gravity and with special allegiance to facts, which is our sufficient apology for introducing the aforesaid "bear story," and all good and loyal Americans are expected to show becoming gratitude therefor. Moreover, we warn all and singular that this chronicle is entrenched behind an impregnable fortress of documents and faithful witnesses, and that it would be a piece of foolhardy recklessness to doubt or question or to meanly "let on," or "if I might be permitted to express a misgiving '—no, sir; this history is not for the faithless and unbelieving, but for you—our glorious elect, who stagger at nothing that contains a bear story! And let us proceed: Mr. James H. Becklow—United States Deputy Marshal, referred to elsewhere in this work—is the only remaining connecting link with these earliest days of "Cantonment Leavenworth." The Deputy was the intimate friend and associate of Sergeant Ellis, one of Col. Leavenworth's men, who in his old age, lived on his pension in the vicinity of the Fort, at Weston, Missouri.

Fort Leavenworth was established for the protection of the Santa Fé traders from the incursions of the Indians who had begun to plunder the caravans passing in yearly increasing numbers over this route. From 1835 to 1845 Col. Dodge, 3d U. S. Dragoons, occupied the Fort, and during the years 1849-50 the years of the great hegira to the California gold fields, 70,000 men, women, and children passed through this reservation to Utah, California, and Oregon.

It is impossible to look coldly down upon ground hallowed by the footprints of the immortals. The flower of the old army spent portions of their service here, and now fill the graves of heroes, or still linger in honorable retirement. Here Col. E. V. Sumner used to bring Sturgis, the athlete, up with a round turn for a slip in his conduct of the company drill, and here it was that Sturgis, too, was wont to meet all comers, barring none, for he was a very Hercules in strength; Gen. Winfield S. Hancock was once Quartermaster at the Fort and afterward Department Commander; Charley May, of Mexican fame; the Steeles; old Braxton Bragg, when he was a subaltern; Canby, since the Civil War, treacherously assassinated in the Lava Beds; Meiggs Quartermaster-General during the Civil War; Stephen W and Phil Kearney; Marcy, Sully, and "Uncle John" Sedgwick, of glorious memory.

Here the Kearney Expedition was organized and set out on their famous march to Lower California in 1846. And from thence Kit

Carson with an escort of fifty volunteers made one of his oft-repeated return journeys to California. Kit at this time (1847) was a lieutenant in the Rifle Corps of the U.S. Army. Here in 1847 Gen. Stephen W. Kearney arrived from California, having with him, John C. Frémont, under arrest for mutinous conduct on the Pacific coast. From thence Maj. John W. Sedgwick, commanding dragoons, operated in the early Kansas troubles, which he survived to become a distinguished leader in the battles of Fredericksburg and The Wilderness, meeting his death at Spottsylvania. Here the dilettante Magruder, in "the days befo' de wah," improvised military pageants for the delectation of the crowd and the emolument of the powder contractor. From thence Gen. Joseph Lane's Expedition to Oregon began their march in 1848, and Captain Stansbury's Expedition to Salt Lake in 1849. From thence the new military road leading west 630 miles to Fort Kearney, to connect with the California and Oregon trails, was constructed in 1850.

Fort Leavenworth was the great frontier depot for the other military posts on the Santa Fé and Oregon routes and the general rendezvous for troops proceeding to western posts.

In 1853 the expedition for the preliminary survey of the route for the Pacific Railway was here organized and proceeded west under Frémont and the Surveyors-General; and here in 1856-7 was organized the great Utah Expedition under Albert Sidney Johnston, with Robert E. Lee as Chief of Staff,—a demonstration gotten up to overawe the refractory Brigham Young and his rebellious Mormon contingent. And here old Parson Kerr, chaplain at the Fort during the Kansas prologue, full of the pro slavery virus, prayed for civil war as a blessing! Here died, in 1858, Gen. Persifer F. Smith, whose remains were conveyed to a steamboat by Gen. Harney with a troop of cavalry, a batallion of infantry, and a section of artillery. An honorary escort of notable officers officiated as pall-bearers on this occasion. This event in the history of the garrison will recall to the loiterers of a past generation the stately and impressive measures of "The Persifer F. Smith March," as given on the piano in the fashionable drawing-rooms throughout the Union in ante-bellum days.

Here the gallant Reno was Ordnance Officer when the guns of Sumter placed the solemn signet of the Lord God upon the death of slavery; here the knightly son of Mars answered to his name, and went quickly to the post of duty. At the capital of the nation he was given a Major-general's commission and a bloody grave at Chantilly!

Custer, whose life went out in bloody eclipse on the Rosebud, was here frequently with the famous 7th Cavalry after the war; and Gen. Philip H. Sheridan had his headquarters here for a short time since the war, and might have remained indefinitely but for a difference which arose between himself and the Recorder touching the limit of fast driving under the city ordinances. The legend goes that both man and quadruped took to cover when they saw "Little Phil" coming down Broadway like an arrow shot from the bow, and objection arose to the introduction of Winchester time over the crossings where women and children were wont to pass, and the local justice subscribed to the prevailing prejudice to the extent of a hundred-dollar fine. This Sir Philip resented in high dudgeon, and his wrath was never appeased, although his friends in the city, as a foil, paid the fine, and followed the matter up by appearing at his headquarters, hat in hand, with apologies done up in tin foil and presented on a gold-lined silver salver, but he would hear none of them, and went down to his grave with his noble rage unplacated; and common folk used to say that for all they knew "he might have been a good general, but on occasion he could be a mighty small man." The general of the army put the finishing touches on his *faux pas* by shaking the dust of the Fort from his military trousers and hied him to the more congenial environment of Chicago, and they do say that this little affair cost the city of Leavenworth a round sum in fat army contracts.

Gen. William T. Sherman, then a captain in the Commissary Department, visited the Fort in 1852 to inspect cattle destined for Col. Sumner's command in New Mexico, and found the Government Reservation then, as now, "a most beautiful spot," but the site of the city of Leavenworth at that time was " a tangled thicket," and there were no whites settled then in this wild Indian country.

The Fort was the temporary seat of the territorial Government in 1854 and here A. H. Reeder, the first Governor of the Territory of Kansas, was welcomed and entertained on his arrival in the autumn of that year

All through the Rebellion the Fort was the base of supplies for the semi-barbarous war of the border, and the plains of the Reservation north of the city, during 1861-5 was the scene of a vast military encampment and here, at the close of the great struggle for the preservation of the Union, on July 1, 1866, at the Government Farm on Logan Avenue, Gen. James H. Lane, U. S. Senator, died the death of the suicide.

*

THE MALL AND ANCIENT BARRACKS.

THE GARRISON GROUNDS.

A lovelier spot for the invalid or pleasure-seeker to while away the long summer days cannot be found in a journey of a thousand miles. The air is pure and exhilarating, the climate mild and equable, and not so exhausting and dangerous to asthmatics and consumptives as the Colorado plains along the base of the Rocky Mountains. Asthma patients at the Hospital of the Western Branch of the National Home, who were doing well here, made the mistake of going to Denver, and died there within two weeks of their arrival, and we believe it to be a mild statement of the truth that the atmosphere here in Leavenworth County is as tonic as that of Colorado without its too often fatal rarefication. The climate here commends itself to all as the true golden mean, and a highly beneficial auxiliary to health-seekers is now supplied in natural salt-water baths through the medium of a convenient and ample natatorium, situated near the Trolley line, on the Reservation.

The garrison avenues, named after eminent soldiers, are lovely promenades, and a fine boulevard leads south from the Fort, through the city, past the grounds of the National Home and on southward, terminating at the Kansas State Prison in Lansing,—a drive altogether of seven miles, or a round trip of fourteen miles.

The Trolley will carry the visitor in a continuous ride over five miles of this route, or ten miles the round trip, and over other miles of the city streets by connecting branches of the same system and all for one fare

"Sheridan's Drive," on the Reservation, is a distinct and romantic rustic serpentine, complete in itself. The route lies along the crest of a chain of hills, or semi-mountains, and affords varied and extensive views of the city, river, valley and far-lying hamlet.

Innumerable fine drives leading past the Reservation and out of the city in every direction lend interest, enjoyment, and recreation to the tired mind and body, and one can easily count a score of falsely celebrated resorts and watering places, which bear no comparison in wheeling attractions—luke or stepper—to the city of Leavenworth and environs. Where on this earth will you go to find a more beautiful pastoral region than the river counties of sunny eastern Kansas? and the chiefest of these is Leavenworth, the fruit center of the Missouri Valley. Take a spin along Salt Creek Valley, or out on the "Stranger," and verify our claim. The tourist, vacation idler, and health-seeker can here find a change from the conventional resort, which has nothing but the dining-room to relieve its utter weariness and ennui

Leavenworth County is a land of orchards, gardens, and vineyards, and while our tables offer a bill of fare second to none we have the shady avenues where lofty elms abound and fruitful fields whose bounties not only satisfy the palate, but spread a glorious prospect to feast the eye. I have stood upon the eminence which sentinel this historic town—Pilot Knob, the elevated table lands of the Salt Creek Range, and the crests of the hills of Lansing—and looked, many a time and oft, upon scenes as exquisitely beautiful as may be seen anywhere in this dear native land of ours! I do not point the reader to sublimity o effect here, but he who in the love of nature stands upon these summits will see the sky bending above outstretched vistas as fair as

"Scotland's red moors and golden burn."

There is no pleasanter spot for the loiterer than the Garrison Grounds during the vernal season. The Main or Central Parade Ground is a beautiful park of shaded green sward, on which is held the Guard Mount every morning in summer, and Dress Parade in the evening. Here the flag-staff and pieces of artillery give token of the military character of the place, and serve as a gentle reminder of the glory and power of the Republic. As we stroll along we see, flashing through the foliage on the opposite side of the square, a troop going through the sword exercise, or a company of infantry drilling in the manual. On the West End Parade are held the battalion and skirmish drills and maneuvers. At the Riding School visitors repair to a private gallery, where they may witness the cavalry drills and exhibitions given daily during the fall and winter months. Daring riders here often perform equestrian feats which rival the professional displays in the Circus Maximus.

The answering bugle calls, the rat-tat of accompanying drums, the quick movements of the sprightly, strong, young braves in their smart uniforms, the sharp word of command, the martial strains of the Military Band, complete a war picture on a "peace footing," further softened by groups of merry children at play, or speeding vehicles crowned with batteries of bright eyes in brave array!

The buildings and improvements on the Reservation cost in the aggregate away beyond the $4,000,000 mark. The barracks are two-story brick structures, with broad verandas extending the length thereof. Here the companies are comfortably housed and enjoy the conveniences of civilized life, including reading-rooms and a good public library. Some of these barracks are quite venerable in appearance, having stood, as now, for a half century or more. There are two places for public worship: an antique Roman Catholic chapel and a very handsome Protestant structure. Some notable buildings have been erected in recent years, among them the new Mess Hall, Gaiety or Amusement Hall, and Schofield Hall, where the officers are quartered. The garrison buildings entire are heated from a central power-

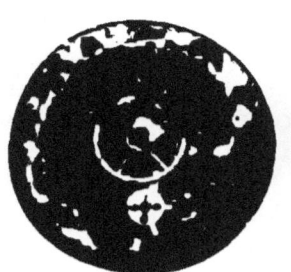

houses, at the National Home the grounds are policed and kept daily and perfect order and cleanliness reigns

The consolidated Mess Hall has a seating capacity of about 1500 This subsidiary dining hall is neatly furnished and the kitchen equipment ranks with the best mod rn conveniences of the kind

Instruction supplementary to that given at West Point is furnished at Fort Leavenworth a School of Application for Cavalry and Infantry A Lieutenant from a post of the to this point every two years. The first class take a course in Military and International Law, Mahan's Outposts, Field Fortification, Signaling and Telegraphy, Operations of War, etc.—everything as taught by the great military masters. The second class are drilled in the common branches, and receive instruction in Field Fortification, Surveying, and Field and Garrison Duty.

At the Military Prison, where trades are taught, and whose inmates erect all the buildings under the supervision of a competent paid foreman, and police the grounds, material worth $250,000 is annually manufactured into boots and shoes, harness, brooms, barrack chairs, etc.; all the needs of the army being met in this way.

One of the most interesting objects on the Garrison Grounds is Taft's colossal statue of Gen. U. S. Grant. It occupies a coign of vantage between Grant and Pope Avenues. On the north face of the granite pedestal, on a bronze tablet, the General and his staff are shown in bas-relief, and on a similar tablet on the south face are the names of the engagements in the Mexican War in which the General participated as a young lieutenant, and where he won his first brevets; and following, the names of his famous victories during the Civil War.

Southwest of the Garrison proper, at the distance of half a mile, lies the National Cemetery, with park grounds adjoining, on which is a permanent speaker's platform for memorial assemblies and exercises. Here, within a substantial stone enclosure, lie the remains of about 3,000 dead, gathered, for the most part, from remote outposts on our frontier, among them five commissioned officers who fell with Custer on the Rosebud, the General's brother Tom being one of them.

Here, in the visible presence of a glorious past, teeming with memories of knightly heroism fast fading into that oblivion which is our destined end and way, we uncover in silent salutation to breathe a prayer for the heroic souls who dared all, who endured all, who gave up all for home and country and flag.

THE CITY OF LEAVENWORTH

was born in 1854. The birth was illegitimate, the offspring of illicit love - of gain. The territory of which the town site is a part passed by purchase, as the reader is aware, from France to the United States, and thence by treaty to the Delaware Indians, who were the owners pledged as such by the inviolable faith of the nation.

The town company was the little toe on the foot of manifest destiny. Whenever the Democratic party undertook to outrage, or succeeded in trampling upon the plighted faith of the Government as declared in the most solemn forms of public law and legal enactment, it was called "manifest destiny." The Leavenworth Town Company was composed of Democrats of the best barb-wire Platte County stripe, to whom it was manifestly the correct thing to squat upon ground owned by others and proceed to survey a town site and to do all and singular pertaining to the evolution of bare-faced highway robbery. The long suffering red man looked on too full for utterance, and the strategic town company took good care to keep him full – of taffy and the worst brand of Kentucky sour till the lands were ceded in due form, and a patent obtained, which took about three years.

The town was originally named "Douglas," in compliment to the contemporary Illinois senator for his burglarious services in breaking down the compromise of 1820, but afterward assumed the nomenclature of the founder of the Fort in the fond hope and expectation that like Cincinnati, Pittsburgh, Chicago and Detroit, which were all built contiguous to forts, the town would prosper and become great and withal become the capital of the Territory. Having driven his stake, the all too fresh pale face set about with commendable energy to build a city. Yesterday there was a tangled thicket, to-day there is a steam-engine in the open excitedly "sawing out its clothes," to become decently clad and composed before some wandering squaw or worse surprise should take it unawares. Four tents bore it company, "all on one street" a barrel of water or whisky on tap, and the dinner-pot on a pole over the fire. It was a condition and not a theory, and the star of empire came and stood over where the young child was, in the form of a tiger sticker, under a cottonwood tree, with his case before him, "busily putting together the first number of the new paper."

The new birth did not escape the eruptions peculiar to infancy, and at a very tender age had a breaking out of the county-seat endemic. The featherless squab called Kickapoo, on the north, with its thirty cabins, signed articles for the race, and the aspiring hamlet once known as Delaware, southward, now in its senile old age a sort of annex to the State Prison graveyard, also put in for the cup.

Leavenworth had about five hundred legal votes, and, in the full assurance of a big majority, laughed to scorn the landings on either side of her. But while she slept the tares grew. Kickapoo had one hundred and fifty *bona fide* voters, but she was up at dawn on election day and a-doing. Her faithful mighty men sent a herald over among the pro-slavery allies in Missouri, and the ferry was kept busy in transferring voters to the Kansas side to support the cause sacred to Kickapoo. The result was a poll of 850 votes. Illustrious Delaware down in the brush on the river bank east of Lansing, moved by the Quaker spirit, got in some fine work also, She had a poll of fifty votes to begin with, and, undismayed, went desperately at work to overcome the odds: hired a steamboat to transfer a competing contingent across the river. She kept the polls open three days, and proclaimed a total cast of 900 ballots. The decision was first given to Kickapoo, on the ground that keeping the polls open for three days was an "unheard-of irregularity" among a people disciplined from the cradle in the fine distinctions of Platte County "law and order." Kickapoo and Delaware died of marasmus, and Leavenworth held a county-seat wake over the remains of her defunct rivals.

In the long ago the Big Muddy, true to its ancient cult, attempted to *chute* in the direction of Santa Fé, New Mexico, anticipating by some years the overland freight route to that point. The great bend at Atchison was the point of departure, but, out of disgust for the name of that town, the Serpentine came to itself and resumed its course toward the Mississippi. Atchison, situated on the outer rim of this detour, has always plumed itself on the fact that it has, in consequence of this crook, twenty miles the start westward of Leavenworth and some sixty miles the bulge on Kansas City. In the early days, when that town was given over to a reprobate mind, on account of an unfortunate christening, she blindly contended that her position westward of her river rivals should give her the prestige of a leader in the Missouri Valley. Fortune hesitated in making this award, but Atchison is right; and if she can hold out, her ambition will be realized, for by the close of the twentieth century she will find herself at the foot of the Rocky Mountains, where she can "go snax" with Denver and become a part of the national infirmary for the distempered per cent of our countrymen.

The exercises are now about to open, so to speak, and I suppose from this year of grace 1854, down through all the years immediately preceding the war and continuing on to the sacking of Lawrence, in 1861, there was more of what old Shag-nasty Jim, of the Lava Beds, would call "fun," more of that beastly, ghastly, border-ruffian hilarity in the town of Leavenworth and the Territory of Kansas to the square yard than on any other spot on earth since the days of Herod the Tetrarch.

Almost everybody that ever was anybody, at some time or other, has taken a hand at molding the clay out of which was formed the commonwealth of Kansas, and as the early history of the city of Leavenworth is so intimately associated with that of the infancy of the Territory, we will survey the retrospect as a whole, for there are many exits and entrances and many figures coming and going on a scene where amity and the softer phases of human intercourse count for little, but where, on the contrary, the fierce hate and savagery of degraded man has been summoned to carry out a deliberate political purpose— that of condemning virgin soil dedicated to freedom to the enslavement of man.

The plot was matured in Washington in 1853, under the patronage of one Pierce, of New Hampshire, now forgotten, but then occupying the White House ; and that part of Missouri known as the Platte Purchase, across the river from Leavenworth, and the home of David R. Atchison and the pugilist Benjamin Franklin Stringfellow, became preeminently the border-ruffian region, or base of operations for the invasion of Kansas   It was on this ground in 1854, at St Joseph, that Stringfellow, in a public speech advocating invasion, said . 'Mark every scoundrel among you who is in the least tainted with abolitionism and exterminate him ' Neither give nor take quarter from the —— rascals.'

Six weeks before the arrival of the first free state colony there was held a pro-slavery convention on Salt Creek in Leavenworth County, which announced that slavery already existed in Kansas and that, under the mild, conciliatory border ruffian rule, Missouri being had shown a close affinity for abolitionists, and that gentlemen of that persuasion would do well to make a note on 't   About this time Benjamin Franklin Stringfellow the dear old sport a mixture of Uncle

Ben Franklin, of Philadelphia, with Sixteen-String Jack, which always hurt me—went on to Washington, and, on the showing that western Missouri had 50,000 slaves worth $25,000,000, demonstrated to the satisfaction of Davis, Toombs & Co. that 2,000 of these slaves placed early on Kansas soil would make a slave State out of it.

William H. Seward, in 1854, from his place in the United States Senate, responded to these threats of the slave power in the following words: "Come on then, gentlemen of the slave States; since there is no escaping your challenge, I accept in behalf of freedom. We will engage in competition for the virgin soil of Kansas, and God give the victory to the side that is strongest in numbers as it is in the right!"

A. H. Reeder, an easy-going, honest, speculating Keystone Dutchman of florid speech, was the first territorial Governor, who arrived at the Leavenworth landing in October, 1854, on the steamer *Polar Star*, a Mississippi boat, which survived the snags and sawyers of our western waters to transport the writer's regiment and another, part of Pope's Army of the Mississippi, from Island No. 10 to the attack upon the rebel works on Chickasaw Bluffs, above Memphis, in the spring of 1862.

The pro-slavery mob which welcomed Reeder, looked upon him as their tool, and anticipated a pic-nic in the work of placing Kansas on the black list. In the pursuit of this purpose there was a gathering of the clans in the early spring of 1855 for the election of members to the Territorial Legislature. Claib Jackson—you remember Claib—the wandering Governor of poor old Missouri in the days when Gen. Nathaniel Lyon was helping her to make up her mind "which way she ought to go": Claib crossed the river with 1,000 men to give the Territory of Kansas the benefit of a neighborly lift at the polls. Claib said, among other things, that "the d—— Yankee —— might vote, but he would do some of the balloting also, and all of the counting." He was as good as his word. When one of his men presented a ballot a judge of the election said: "Are you a resident of Kansas?" "Yes." When the judge persisted: "Does your family live in Kansas?" The border ruffian drew his revolver and answered: "—— you! that is none of your business," and added, shoving his gun into the judge's face: "I want you to git out o' here, or I'll blow — out of you." The judges vacated the premises without ceremony, and there was a beastly majority in that precinct for the pro slavery candidate. Atchison, Stringfellow & Co. participated also in these festivities, and brought with them in

all about 5,000 of Platte County perfectionists to see that ' Law and
order" prevailed outside of Missouri, since there was so little of it at
home   This pro slavery missionary force were becomingly adorned
with "Arkansaw" tooth picks whisky, and whatever other warlike material lay at hand, to which additions were made from the stock of aboli
tionists as opportunity presented itself.   One enterprising Yankee in
Leavenworth County bestirred himself to counter the Blue Lodge
method of carrying the election in his precinct, and sought the neigh
boring lodges of the red man for votes, whereupon the following esti
mate of the relative merits of Yankees and Pukes was evolved   ' Good
man — heap — Yankee town. Missouri — bad — heap — heap — heap — d —
um."   Being further pressed for a decision in favor of the applicant,
the Indian retired for a confab with his braves, and at length came out
and said   "Tinkum four days — den vote heap — heapum — some time
— maybe ! "

    The bulldozed judges of election meekly accepted the voice of
Missouri at the Kansas polls as the voice of ' manifest destiny, ' whilst
Atchison. Stringfellow & Co. whacked the pine counters of the doggeries with their fists till they resounded again ; filled high the flowing
bowl, and drank damnation to all enemies of the slave power whom
soever. The fraudulent poll for members of the Legislature awoke the
free-state men to the true situation, and William Phillips, of Leaven
worth, a respected attorney and property-holder in good circumstances,
a man of earnest convictions, but of quiet demeanor and orderly
deportment, was active, in concert with other good and true men in
framing and presenting a petition to Gov. Reeder to have the election
set aside, which was done, or partially so, and Phillips was ever there
after a mark for pro slavery vengeance. In those days there stood at the
corner of Cherokee and Main Streets, near the landing, an old elm tree,
in whose ample shade out-door public assemblies were wont to be held
Here, during the excitement prevailing over the unsettled election, a
crowd came together for a general reckoning of election scores, the set
tlement of conflicting ownership of claims incidentally, and to discuss
the unfinished business of the town, which embraced personal animosi-
ties, political and otherwise, and doggery quarrels of every description
And it may as well be understood at once that if whisky as a potential
factor could have been eliminated from the proceedings of this meeting, and from the entire history of the town down to the present hour,
life would be more tolerable and the flow of blood much less than it

has been. A crowd of Missouri toughs organized the meeting and made rulings to suit their own purposes as each item of business came before them. Among the number present was a young free-state man from Vermont—Cole McCrea by name—a fearless, alert, determined man, below the medium size; who had a claim in dispute, which was being ruled upon adversely to him. This he resented in the usual Western style, and the lie passed, and Malcolm Clark, the leader of the pro-slavery party and chairman of the meeting, rushed upon McCrea, who shot him dead, and another would have been killed, but he stumbled and fell over a sand-bank, and the ball intended for him passed over his head. McCrea, stunned by a blow on the head from behind, ran, dazed, and jumped to the armpits into the river, where he was captured and held under guard while preparations went on for hanging him, which would have been done but for the timely arrival of a company of dragoons, which took him to the Fort and placed him in confinement. McCrea escaped from the Fort and returned east, but made his appearance on the streets of Leavenworth again in 1859. A reward of $2,000 had been offered for him by the bogus Legislature, and he was arrested and jailed, but the free-state men of the town, no longer terrorized by the bushwhackers of the island and the eastern shore, got out the old Kickapoo cannon and went down to the jail and released him. McCrea, advanced in years, is now a member of the Western Branch of the National Home.

William Phillips, aforesaid, attended and probably participated in a quiet way in the meeting under the elm-tree, and was charged, through malice, with being an accomplice of McCrea's, and was ordered to leave town. Leavenworth at this time was a nest of the frontier criminal class, where indiscriminate robbery and murder and the proscription of free-state men were the chief concern and pastime. One Lyle, a member of the pro-slavery gang, but who claimed to be a friend of Phillips and who often enjoyed his hospitality, found him working in his garden one day and engaged his attention while a confederate approached and seized his coat hanging on the fence, which contained his revolver. A mob in waiting came up at the instant and hustled their victim into a boat and pulled to the Missouri shore; thence he was taken to Weston, the ferry-crossing above the Fort, where he was barbarously mal-treated; stripped, one side of his head shaved, and his body tarred and feathered; then he was ridden on a rail through the town to the music of old tin pans and cow-bells, and finally

put on the auction-block and sold by a "nigger" for one cent—after
this fashion. "How much, gentlemen, for a full blooded abolitionist,
dyed in the wool; tar, feathers, and all! How much, gentlemen? he'll
go at the first bid." He was taken, finally, to an old pork house on
the river bank, where the more vicious in the crowd proposed to hang
him. There were a few free state men in the town, and other humane
people not in sympathy with the mob, who began to gather, led by
citizen Wood, a resolute man, armed, through whose interference,
mainly, Phillips was rescued and sent home.

It is said of one Johnson, who was one of this mob, a man of some
education, and, when sober, not devoid of the instincts of a gentleman,
when he came to himself, an accusing conscience lashed the whisky
brave till he cried for shame!

This outrage, however, according to the Leavenworth *Herald*,
sent "a thrill of delight through the community!" And at a public
meeting in the town the act was approved in a set of resolutions.

During the year 1855 the young town adjoining the Fort advanced
rapidly in population and in political and business importance. The
great Government Overland Transportation Company of Majors, Rus-
sel & Co., made their headquarters here, and invested large capital in
an extensive plant. They built store-houses, blacksmith shops, wagon
and repair shops, employing altogether several thousand men. They
had in active use over 500 of their immense freight wagons, 7,000
work cattle and during this year handled 8,000,000 pounds of freight.
These great, broad tired, covered freight-wagons carried about 6,000
pounds each, and were propelled by six to eight yoke of oxen under
the control of Mexican bullwhackers, whose whips of ox hide bellied
as large as a man's wrist and gave forth a report like a rifle-shot. In
the wake of these enterprises followed the freight-wagons of the Salt
Lake and California traders who had large capital invested and who
gave employment to a large number of men. And the Government
withal during these years was disbursing $900,000 per annum for mili-
tary supplies.

Capricious fortune lavished her bounty upon the town throughout
this memorable year, and business reached its climax to ebb there-
from in the "Presidential year" following

But politics and not business is what concerns us for the moment.
One of the Leavenworth gang when assured that Reeder had ordered
a supplementary election as a remedy for the frauds of the first, wanted

3—

to tickle the Governor's throat with a toothpick, and, beyond doubt, this purpose was contemplated in the councils of the desperate men who thronged the doggeries along the landing in 1855. Their leader, the pugilist and bully, Benj. Fr. Stringfellow, attempted to assault the Governor, and would have done so but for the interference of Judge Halderman.

The bogus Legislature, as finally determined at the polls, met on the 2d day of July, 1855.

In the estimation of many on both sides the year seemed marked by special visitation of the judgments of the Almighty—in these things: the bogus Legislature, a drouth of unexampled severity, and the arri. val in the Territory of Jim Lane! The pro-slavery and free-state champions who still linger superfluous receive the mention of this year with a certain suggestive shrug, as much as to say, "That was nearly ——, wasn't it?" And it is still a matter of doubt as to who got the best of these afflictions. In due time the Legislature came together at Pawnee, a spot on the prairie in which Gov. Reeder was financially interested, a fact which gave occasion to old unrecon- structed Bob Toombs, on the floor of the Senate, to say that the Leg- islature had moved to Reeder's town from the town of somebody else at the invitation of the fellow who for the time being made the best bid. The leaders of both sides were on the make, and as a subsidiary source of murder in the new Territory the insane desire to dispossess the squatter of his holdings is entitled, beyond question, to high rank.

Brewerton says that when he made his first call on Gov. Shannon, at the Shawnee Mission, his excellency and the Secretary, Woodson, were reported absent at Lecompton, "staking out claims." As an illus- tration of how the public interests were sacrificed to personal schemes, the story is told of old Judge Lecompte that he could not hold the spring term of court, because he had to plant potatoes; neither could he hold the summer term, because he had to hoe his potatoes; and as for the fall term, must he not dig his potatoes? and the winter term, he insisted, should be side-tracked so he could sell his potatoes. This thrifty old Marylander nursed his "spuds" to some purpose, for, while he was an indifferent lawyer, and a disgrace to the bench, he managed to keep pace with the Yankee in the race for large possessions, and this we consider high praise. He had a stake in every town in the Territory, and owned one of the best claims in Leavenworth County, with a lien of some sort or other on twenty others.

But to return to Pawnee and the first territorial Legislature The members drifted there in prairie schooners, in open wagons, on foot, mounted, all with a grub stake, for they would have none of Reeder's capital, nor his friends' boarding-houses, but stopped obstinately in the "breaks" and "put up"

There have been legislatures and legislatures in this land of political originals, but here is a legislature dropped down on the gravel like a prairie-dog town, and like the conies, the members are racing about in the open, among their tinpans, kettles, and corn meal, barking, shrugging their shoulders at the legislative chaos, diving out of sight betimes and coming forth again with a piece of bacon in one hand and a frying-pan in the other. Here is a member—a Missouri stalwart—candidate for Speaker ; one of the great unwashed, a dirty, greasy, malodorous bushwhacker. The fumes of frying bacon rise to his grateful nostrils ; the coffee boils ; the corn-dodger is sicklied o'er with the pale cast peculiar to the leaden hoe-cake mixed with water only. And now if the very honorable Jones (was ever Jones found missing at the birth of empires?) can find a piece of rosin soap - that old-time mechanical abstergent, Jones will gallantly attempt to swab his face by laying both hands hard upon his noble brow to find them slip suddenly to his chin, and there stick like a porous plaster. Jones perseveres and takes up his pewter-covered pocket mirror to survey the result. He finds the skin gone in patches and dark lines of grime showing the boundaries, possibly, between Kansas and Colorado, and other lines, marking the course of the Kaw and Missouri rivers and the settlers' camps atwixt. Jones takes a second severe glance at his illuminated nose. "Can't see why it won't do," he said, and summarily dismissed his lingering doubt by adding with emphasis, "D—— the soap anyway" But mind you, it was a bright and shining feather in the caps of this Legislature that they had soap with them' One is only fairly judged by the age in which he lived, and his environment and the first territorial Legislature of Kansas compared favorably with the Congress of the United States in the nebulous period " befo' de wah ' when the rules of the code were considered binding, and the junitor's diurnal harvest was enriched by assorted sizes of flasks fished out from under the benches, and the cuspidors were subjected to flagrant neglect accurately gauging the parliamentary refinement of those piping times

The pro-slavery party of Leavenworth were murderously strenuous in their opposition to the effort to organize a territorial govern-

ment on the free-state basis, and denounced the elections proclaimed
by Governor Reeder to fill places declared vacant through fraud at
the polls, and in Leavenworth, on their own ground, the menace was
so strong that the polls were not opened. Provision instead was made
at Easton, twelve miles west. The roads to that point were, however,
patrolled by Leavenworth bushwhackers and the Kickapoo Rangers,
and the free-state men were overawed, and for the most part silenced.
A few of them, indeed, persisted against odds.

Capt. R. P. Brown, a zealous free-state man, and a few others,
defended the polls. There were collisions between the opposing par-
ties, and one Cook, of the pro-slavery faction, was killed during the
night following the election. The next morning Capt. Brown and a
few friends attempted to return home, near Leavenworth. This gallant leader in the cause of free Kansas was a school-teacher by profession, a Christian, and a man of courage; one of those men of humble
origin, thoroughly devoted to the cause of free government, and fated
to martyrdom for a principle; a man of peaceful purposes and meth-
ods, who stood for the truth and his rights under the forms of law,
and who could not be moved to trespass upon another for personal
gain; a clean man, who wished well of his fellow, and the best that
may be for his own hearthstone. Young—life was before him!
Married—wife and child loved and needed him! Poor—these hands
must minister to his necessities, and all he asked was a chance! But
he loved his country, and his country demanded that he exercise the
right of a freeman. May he do this? May he go to the ballot-box
unmolested and assert his manhood? Who are these men who call
themselves Democrats and deny to this man the exercise of his birthright under the stars and stripes? Having proceeded along the road
a few miles, they were intercepted by a force of Kickapoo Rangers
under Capt. Martin; there was an exchange of shots, but the opposing
force largely outnumbered them, and Captain Brown being assured of
fair treatment, his small squad was disarmed and taken back to Easton,
where a mock trial was entered upon. Martin, the leader of the Rangers, to do him justice, made some effort to prevent the shedding of blood
and allowed Brown's friends to escape, but he himself was detained
as a prisoner under constant and momentarily increasing threats from
a drunken crowd of low scoundrels fitly influenced by a persistent
ruffian by the name of Gibson. Brown asked the privilege to defend
himself against their picked man, which was refused. He then offered

to fight any two or three of them, an offer which the cowards would not accept. The drunken savages then fell upon him, and in the struggle for his life the brave man was cut down with a hatchet, the blow cleaving the skull. In the biting cold of a Siberian winter the mortally wounded man was driven over the frozen ground in an open wagon to his home. On the way a wretch, still living in Leavenworth, opened the wound and spat tobacco-juice into it, saying, with an oath, that "that was good enough for a —— abolitionist." He lived three hours after being dragged like a cast off carcass and thrown into the open doorway of his home in the presence of his wife and child, and died on the 18th of January, 1856.

To anticipate a little: in the autumn of this year, when the sumac was red and the sorghum sap sputtered in the vat, and old John Brown began to look about for something to cover his toes, which were sticking through his boots, the boys came out of the brush to wound Shannon, the next in succession as Governor of the Territory. They had their guns well in hand and each of them a battery of small arms and the usual knife – a pungent, purple-top crowd of toughs from poor old Missouri, a State lying far north of the cotton belt, and palsied with a labor system unsuited to her climate and environment. One of the Committee on Reception, in a suit of store clothes, secured in installments from the aggregate ownership of the vicinage, advanced, saluted the new ruler, and began a mellifluous exordium, in which he prayed his excellency to compose himself. "Be persuaded," he said, "that you are now in soft Padua, the Italy of America; that in the ancestral halls of Baron Brown of Osawatomie, and among the pomegranate groves of Bull Creek, Jim Lane will take care of you if Titus and his retainers don't. In this peaceful vale," he continued, "the morning prayer is heard on every hill; the evening orison is chanted in every glen." One would infer from the style of the welcome, that these truly great and incorruptible Democrats closed the exercises by celebrating holy mass followed by the doxology and benediction in due form: but they didn't do anything of the kind. They went over to the refreshment counter and took a drink of straight Kentucky corn and had it chalked.

On the outskirts of the crowd, which overflowed the building and lounged upon the sward outside, a lean and hungry Cossack of the frontier had his bowie hard on the grindstone, putting a wire-edge on it, while a litter of like whelps sprawled on the ground hard by, "waiting," as they said, "to pull the gizzard out of some ——— abolitionist."

The unwonted intrusion of mean whiskey upon the scene of the '50s in Kansas compels us to revert at this point to the only speech delivered by David R. Atchison, which survives to illumine Kansas annals and to shed lustre upon the career of the Platte County apostle of the slave power. The trick peculiar to Satan, to decoy his victim to the top of a mountain, where the temptation might be as conspicuous and spectacular as possible, was employed here, and the noble David (who, by an accident which he always esteemed as special proof of the divine favor, became during the interregnum of one Sunday President of the United States) ascended Mount Oread and delivered himself of the following strain of fiery persiflage :

"I am a Kickapoo Ranger, by ——! Be gallant to the ladies, but if you find one armed, trample her under foot as you would a snake, and if anybody resists, show 'em no quarter. And now we will support our highly honorable Jones and test the strength of that —— Free-state Hotel. Be brave! and if any man or woman stands in your way, blow 'em to —— with a chunk of cold lead!"

It is hardly worth while to state what happened when the valiant David descended from the mount, and at short range fired his cannon at the hotel. The result would have been the same had he aimed at the Rocky Mountains. You can't aim a gun with both eyes open, although you are steadied with the best Kentucky ballast, unless those orbs are "sot" like Ben Butler's, who could hit the bull's-eye with his left and calmly measure calico with his right, all in one time and one motion.

Speaking of center shots reminds me of an old-timer of the '50s. You may remember him—Dick Richardson—a member of the H. R.; old Dick Richardson, of Quincy, Illinois; the contemporary, friend, and tool of Douglas. He was a fair sample of the pro-slavery M. C. in ante-bellum days. Dick started on his political career tall, young, and fair, with some brains and a host of friends, but whisky finished him, as it brought to a premature close the life of his great political mentor, and another contemporary as well—a brilliant war governor— all of the gallant old Sucker State. For how many generations has man been confessing to himself: What a harvest King Alcohol has gathered!

Dick had a fashion, in his later and grosser years, of sitting down to talk with an old crony, perchance with a stranger just introduced—anybody—no matter ; and as he sat confronting you, his good-natured face beaming at the recollection of a good story which he soon began to spin, the compound fluid extract of the weed oozing from the corners of his mouth and falling at intervals on his shirt front and thence in a sort of spray or bridal-veil leaps down his vest to his trousers,—eminently pictorial and reminiscent was Richard! But now, look ye ' The old-time box of saw-dust, dark with the expectorations of a generation and deeply layered with the quids of an extinct race, might be in sight or not, it was an unrecognized forerunner of better things at the utmost, and subject to continual protest and martyrdom as such. And Dick had a nimble and experienced pucker and a reckless way of squirting tobacco-juice that kept his interlocutor in a state of deplorable and often frenzied incertitude and apprehension, nor did the wretched man always escape extreme catastrophe for which Dick made (as he conceived) the most generous and ample amends by pressing his victim to the trough for a hot sling

But let us get back to our muttons, which we can easily do, for the distance from Quincy to Leavenworth is not great.

We are now well along in the year 1856, and in the streets of Leavenworth, where the pro-slavery crusaders from every Southern State have gathered like maggots in a dunghill, taken possession of the town, and are patrolling the streets after their own fashion, terrorizing the people.

Emory's gang of road agents led the dance of death Whether this leader had personal knowledge of all the crimes perpetrated in his name cannot now be definitely determined. That the pro-slavery press cried ' War ''' and that there was a preconcerted campaign of plunder and murder, is indisputable. Geary, the pro-slavery appointee, himself testifies to the reign of terror, and says, describing the aspect of the town, that the landing on his arrival was covered with drunken loafers asleep on the heads of whisky barrels, that armed horsemen were dashing about in every direction, companies were drilling, and a confused picture of rattling sabers, beating drums, and playing fifes was presented to his view Horse-stealing was the only industry of the town that took precedence of the military and the Regulators, who called themselves militia, secured their mounts in large measure in that deft way. A stranded refugee, standing in front of Gen Smith's headquarters at the Fort saw his horses being driven through the

grounds to a loaded wagon by a Missouri freebooter, and, with the help
of the military, stopped the team, unhitched the span, and took them
away, leaving the wagon in the road.

The old Lawrence road, leading round the foot of Pilot Knob, was
the scene of many dark crimes. It was on this highway, on the outskirts of the town, that the wretch Fugit shot young Hoppe, returning quietly in his carriage from Lawrence, scalped his victim, and carried off his trophy to decide a wager he had made of $6 against a pair
of boots that within two hours he would return to the doggery with
the evidence of his victory in his hand.

On this road Major Sackett, of the U. S. Army, during the reign
of terror in this year of grace 1856, discovered the mutilated bodies
of thirteen men slain from ambush or taken unawares openly, being
unarmed.

Through the streets armed horsemen rode, blowing horns and
ordering free-state men to leave the town on pain of death, and for
days indiscriminate outrage prevailed—dwellings and stores were pil-
laged, and men, women, and children in scores, without sufficient money
or clothing, were driven aboard steamboats and out of the Territory.

Those who were specially marked for vengeance were hunted to
the river bank or into the thickets and shot down. Against the
defenseless people these ruffians levied war, instead of marching to
meet Jim Lane, of whom they had a wholesome terror.

A single whisper of Lane's approach was enough to send these
drunken braggarts into hiding, nor did they wait upon the order for
their retreat, but disappeared at a plunge, like scared rats. They were
often flushed in this way; the sound of a going in the tops of the
mulberry trees or the hollow note of affrighted warning brought a sud-
den and death-like quiet to the streets of Leavenworth. A sepulchral
silence reigned in the doggeries about Second and Third streets, the
guilty leaders slunk out of sight, and the more venturesome, who met
like ghosts in the shadows, talked with bated breath. To the haunted
imaginations of these lurking lazzaroni hell was a nap on a flower bank
in the Elysian Fields compared to a visit from Jim Lane and his gallant
lieutenants, Mark Parrott and H. Miles Moore. Here were men,
now gathered with Lane at Lecompton, who had been driven out of
Leavenworth under the menace of a noose and a short shrift, and who
thirsted to return and try conclusions with the brigands. Given an
open field and a fair fight, there would beyond doubt have been a b'oody

encounter at this juncture, but the free-state men were overawed by the presence of the strong arm of the Government at the Fort, and Lane wisely refused the stormy and urgent demands of his followers to march north.

Lane is still an uncanny recollection among the mossy antiques of Platte County, who never got over the fits of jim-jams with which Jim afflicted the wicked in and out of Leavenworth in the days that are no more, and will no more return.

One of the precautions which Eastou, Emory & Co. took against a surprise by Lane was a cordon of freight-wagons which they drew across what they supposed was the most vulnerable approach to the town, and on the Lawrence road one night they placed a picket or cavalry vidette of twenty men on the extreme outpost, under an experienced Mexican veteran, whose valorous example it was believed would nerve the Platte County volunteers and Kickapoo members of the "law and order" guard and inspire them to "stick" against all comers. The captain, speaking reminiscently of this matter, says the men rode out to their sanguinary work with great confidence, and indeed were given to loud and vaporous epithets against the foe, and indulged in no little commiseration for the misguided people who could be so weak and desperately idiotic as to attack them in their Leavenworth stronghold. Was not the gifted warrior, Davy Atchison, close at hand? And the very eminent Benj. Fr. Stringfellow, is he not at our backs, couchant? And the distinguished doggery-keeper, Dunn are not his sleepless energies at our call? And the broad cuffs and immaculate ruffles of H. Rives Pollard, are not these impregnable against any attack which the enemy can make? Ha' ha' and they passed the bottle and yelled, 'Let the —— Yankee paupers come on.' And so by night, in the covert of the thicket off Pilot Knob, they took their stand and midnight came apace and spectral silence, and the rabbit's tread started vague fears and the suspicious and wary sentinels shrank within deeper shadows and listened, and the mocking winds gave passing sneers and there were apprehensions to quiet, and a certain fearful looking out upon "the front" that was not reassuring

What is that?' whispered Jack to Tom, across the road and the screech-owl laughed a hollow laugh out of the near by tree tops, so much as to say, 'Look out they're coming!' And now there were mysterious rallies by twos and threes, and by the pale moonlight there was the glint of a flask and a soft gurgle and an aroma of distilled

corn stole out upon the night air. But it was no use; a sound dead-
lier than before came from down the road. The more timid already
had one foot in the stirrup. " 'Tis nothing," the captain said, " but a
belated traveler, or the browsing cattle." " But I heard the ' sicken-
ing thud ' of advancing hoofs," they said, and " Lane, by God ! " they
cried in chorus, and it takes time to write the fact down, but those
gentlemen made the grand entry within the walls of the city in about
one and a quarter, by Professor John O'Day's watch.

During the years intervening between 1852 and 1860 there was a
brace of figure-heads in Washington, known in the idiom of the common people as Frank Pierce and Old Buck, who operated a political
machine designed apparently for turning out governors for the Territory of Kansas. It was a sort of " short-order " device—everybody by
turns, and nobody long, at the pie counter. In this way it came to
pass that John W. Geary succeeded Shannon, and I do not know how
many other fellows, as Governor, and landed in Kansas September 9,
1856, and sat right down and fired a letter back to Old Buck saying
that "the town of Leavenworth is now in the hands of armed bodies
of men, who, having been enrolled as militia, perpetrate outrages of
the most atrocious character under the shadow of authority from the
territorial Governor." And adds " that desolation and ruin reign
everywhere, and families have even sought protection with the Indian
tribes." Whereupon Jeff. Davis, the dear old patriot, as Secretary of
War, writes to Gen. P. F. Smith, in command at the Fort, authorizing
him to call upon the Government for militia "to suppress and crush the
rebellion in Kansas." This was very good for a starter, and to keep
things red hot, and as a sort of condition precedent to putting down
the rebellion, a festival of devils was forthwith introduced into Leavenworth as already hinted at and which will be further touched upon
as truth demands. As a precaution, Joe Shelby, in the exercise of
self-constituted supervisory powers over Kansas, with a force of the
unterrified, stood picket on the outposts at Lexington, where he
boarded every up-bound steamboat, and interrogated, bulldozed, and
searched every passenger suspected of holding political opinions at
variance with his own, and Platte County zealots engaged in a similar
service at Leavenworth. Moreover, a self-appointed vigilance committee took charge of the town, to rescue the people, as they gravely
asserted, from the grasp of the " Emigrant Aid Paupers," bearing
Sharpe's rifles. This vigilance committee had its origin in the

Masonic Lodge of Leavenworth, whose councils the pro-slavery members prostituted to the furtherance of their political and murderous intrigues. Here it was that Phillps's death was secretly canvassed, and here the pro-slavery party of the town came to the parting of the ways, and such men as H. Miles Moore, no longer willing to be made a tool of the slave-holding oligarchy, abandoned their councils, and cast their lot henceforth with the free-state men. The streets of the town were given up to a hostile army of Rangers, 800 strong, under Emory, a Maryland slaveholder, by birth and breeding a gentleman, but the tool of an odious conspiracy, and as such came into malign prominence, and tarries an unregarded figure among the cast-off masks and worthless toggery of the gruesome revelers of 1856

On Sunday night, September 1, 1856, Emory's gang of drunken cut-throats paraded the streets, bent on forcing a bloody issue. The doggeries seethed with a mass of armed assassins, who spoke in under tones and exchanged significant glances. Not all of them understood the secret and sworn purpose already decided upon, but there was something in the wind, and the crowd of bullies who did not share the councils of their leaders were kept well in hand to execute whatever crime was pointed out to them, and to receive as their reward the privilege of being hanged instead of their principals if this was to be the outcome, which possibility seemed remote enough The next day, September 2d, the Regulators, under Emory, after committing many outrages, approached the house of William Phillips, who had suffered at the hands of a mob in May of the preceding year, as already detailed in these pages. The home of this martyr to our free institutions is still a comfortable abode, on Shawnee Street, nearly opposite the opera house To this point the mob of mounted brigands rode up. Phillips had a perfect understanding of his own situation during all the turbulent months of this memorable year, and in the face of repeated warnings, bravely met his fate. We may well believe he felt a secret shame at the very thought of flight Why should he retreat? Here was his home He stood upon his birthright to live the life of a worthy, useful citizen, obedient to the laws and under the very shadow of the flag of his country Once out from under his own roof, whither should he go? To the river bank, to be shot down like a wild beast as had been the fate of others? Are home and all vested rights to be sacrificed in an hour to the behests of the commune? Is this the boasted liberty of the Republic? Whither shall

•

SCENE OF THE PHILLIPS TRAGEDY ON SHAWNEE ST. OPPOSITE OPERA HOUSE.

he go? The memory of wrongs already borne had sunk deep into his soul. He will defend his life and his hearthstone to the last. A brother is the only friend with him in his extremity. As the mob advanced upon his ground, open trespassers under the law upon the most sacred rights, they confessed to the world that they were outlaws, and without excuse or defense of any kind. Phillips stood within at a window, gun in hand, and as his enemies came on he took the initiative, clearly within his right, and fired, killing two of them. There was an answering volley and the patriot and hero died where he stood, and his brother lost an arm. A street full of armed men against one, but

         "'T was a famous victory."

A singular incident connected with the death of Phillips is related of his wife, a lovely and accomplished woman. Having for a year endured the tumult, apprehension, and dangers which surrounded her and her husband, her mind became affected, and she had been removed to an asylum in Iowa, and when the messenger arrived to announce the death of her husband, by a strange premonition she anticipated him and said in a natural and composed tone of voice, "William is dead; I heard him fall!'"

It is worth while here to trace the events which fix the responsibility and stamp with infamy the memory of the men who were the prime cause of the death of William Phillips. The *canaille* who mobbed him in '55 and shot him down in '56 were at most mere tools and accessories. The town of Weston, above the Fort, during the years aforesaid was the principal trade-center and steamboat landing of this immediate region. Here was the ferry where the California hegira crossed in '49, '50. Like Grant's base on the James, Weston was Atchison, Stringfellow & Co's Missouri River base for the invasion of Kansas. Here, at the old St. George Hotel, swarmed the law-yers, speculators, politicians, gamblers, adventurers and cut-throats of the frontier, and here, along the principal street, the One Sunday President of the United States was wont to ride up in front of String-fellow's office, and drop the bridle rein and his morning salutation 'Well Ben, what's the news?' Here these leaders laid their plans and employed such tools in their execution as they found most efficient, among these was the political stallion in charge of the Platte County *Argus*, whose chief end was to whoop 'em up and give voice to the pro-slavery campaign. Here the Jacobin Club, known as the "Self-Defensives," held its secret oath-bound meetings, where David R. Atchison administered the oath. And here in this town it was that Rev. Frederick Starr was tried by an improvised, self-constituted court having neither legal sanction nor jurisdiction, on three charges, to wit:

1st. "That he taught negroes to read."

2d. "That he proposed to a slave to buy his freedom."

3d. "That he was seen riding in an open buggy with a negro domestic."

There was a buzzing among the ladies present when the last charge was read, but the reverend gentleman made a vigorous defense, and was so blameless in his general walk and conversation that his

enemies acquitted him in open court; with a mental reservation, however, and through a base pretense he was finally driven out of the
State, an innocent man suffering for opinion's sake.

The action of William Phillips to have the 30th of March elections partially declared invalid through the perfectly lawful and
peaceable process of a sworn affidavit presented to Gov. Reeder, dis-
jointed the necks of Atchison, Stringfellow & Co., at Weston, and the
henchman in the *Argus* office set up a roar at his own friends in Leavenworth for their political delinquencies and general worthlessness as
true "law and order" men.   The *Argus* opened a fusilade of dirty
shot-guns on Pollard and Adams, of the Leavenworth *Herald*, and
ceased not its nagging : " There cannot be a true friend of the South,"
said the *Argus*, " in a town where such a traitor as Phillips is permitted to live." This direct appeal to murder and assassination was kept
up for months—until the snowy shirt-ruffles of H. Rives Pollard, of
"Ole Vuhginny," became deeply agitated. At first the response was
feeble, and the *Herald* contented itself with the reply that " there were
circumstances over which it had no control," etc.   The *Argus* plied
the lash, and in due time H. Rives Pollard and Wm. H. Adams, in
charge of the *Herald* office, set their drag-net and gathered in from
the town doggeries a sufficient mob to kidnap Phillips and take him
to Weston, where he was " shamefully entreated," as already described.

The pro-slavery party in Leavenworth, through its Missouri allies,
were so largely preponderant that the free-state men were practically
at their mercy, and Phillips was without support either in the crude
and biased administration of the law or in the popular sentiment, and,
emboldened by their first success with Phillips, they felt secure in their
purpose to murder him when the hour was ripe for the deed.   And
they did not have long to wait : the year 1855 closed speedily, and the
year 1856 rose like a mailed warrior, his lance poised, and his omin-
ous blood-red shield *en banc*, with his heel upon the neck of Phillips,
whom we pronounce in the name of Christ our Lord as true a martyr
to the rights of man as ever lived.

I cannot rid my thought of these two martyrs of the common
people—Captain R. P. Brown and William Phillips, both of whom
died at the hands of the foes of free government in Leavenworth
County in the year of grace 1856.   The icy blasts of forty winters,
save one, have swept their forgotten graves, but if these unconscious heroes rise not in the hearts of our people to a glorious immor-

tality, then is our faith in free government vain; our boasted liberty
an empty sound; patriotism under the stars and stripes a hateful fable,
a mocking pretense. We, of this generation, may be apostate in our
feelings and recreant to the trust committed unto us by the fathers—
be it so—we are persuaded the hearts of our children will not be so
dead to a lesson and example which we ignore.

Is life, then, a fool's masquerade, or do we go forward under a
sense of the avenging judgments of God. So? Then let us honor
these men and execrate the memory of the wild beasts which robbed
the innocent and helpless of their natural protectors, and liberty of
two of her best beloved!

If man was once a god, sinless, and fell to the abyss of devils,
and is now struggling back through redemptive grace to his lost estate,
then we have here - in this bloody offering upon the altar of our liberties—one of those examples by which he profits and through which
we may hope the race beholds, not only its weakness, but its divinely
bestowed inherent power, and from which it can take courage to fight
the good fight which shall crown it with victory!

The scourge of open crime passed gradually away after the lynch-
ing of Quarles and Bayes—the two river thieves and cut-throats—by
the citizens *en masse* in 1857. These illustrious toughs were displayed
to advantage from the limb of a big elm-tree near an old saw mill on
the "run," near where the stove foundries now stand.

Lyle, the tool who betrayed Phillips into the hands of the mob
in 1855, met a deserved fate by being cut to the heart in the open
street and others of the old gang of debauched loafers and blacklegs
passed hence after a similar fashion.

We are fain to drop the curtain on this and kindred horrors, the
fifties sank slowly into the gloom of civil war, the slave power had
played and lost in Kansas, and, glowering with rage and defeat had for
a time to conspire against the life of the Republic.

Those who were quick to discern signs saw blood on the moon
after 1860, and the Slaveholders' Rebellion showed its colors early at
Leavenworth On the morning of April 18, 1861, following the fall
of Sumter, the steamer *Sam Gaty*, the regular St. Louis packet, landed
at Leavenworth flying the rebel flag from her jack staff. The loyal
Germans of the town members of the Turners rallied to resent the
insult, and while they were getting out the "Old Kickapoo," field
piece, the officers of the boat rather than attempt to stand against the

aroused loyalty of the city, hauled down the Confederate rag, and were compelled to surrender it and to fly the colors of the Union.

The steamer *Russell*, the next to appear, was forced to fly "Old glory" before she was permitted to land; the crowd cheered, and Leavenworth henceforth took her rightful place as a staunch defender of the Union.

The city has to her credit a long list of gallant officers and soldiers who achieved fame on the historic fields of the Civil War. Among them Powell Clayton, who entered the service as captain of Company G, First Kansas Infantry, and left the service a brigadier-general, and afterward represented the State of Arkansas in the U. S. Senate.

Dan McCook was first commissioned as captain of the Shields Guards, stationed at the Fort, and afterward commissioned as captain of Company H, First Kansas Infantry. Subsequently he commanded a brigade in the Second Division, Fourteenth Army Corps, Army of the Cumberland, and received a mortal wound in a charge before Marietta, near Kenesaw, June 27, 1864. Hampton P. Johnson was killed in action at Morristown, Mo., September 17, 1861. The last words of this gallant officer were: "Come on, boys!" His body was brought home and buried with military honors. Thomas Moonlight was mustered into the U. S. service as captain of the Leavenworth Light Battery, which was afterward named Company D, and became a part of the Fourth Kansas Infantry. At the close of the war Col. Moonlight commanded the Eleventh Kansas Infantry, and was breveted brigadier-general. Colonel Charles R. Jennison and Lieutenant-Colonel Dan. R. Anthony were officers of the famous First Kansas Cavalry, which rendered conspicuous services to the Government. This regiment afterward became the Seventh Kansas Volunteers—the celebrated "Jayhawkers." To recite the personal history of Colonel Dan R. Anthony would be to give almost a complete epitome of the town of Leavenworth from the day of its birth. 'T is true that after looking over the ground in 1854, he retired, permitting the stormy interval of 1855–1856 to pass before again venturing west of the Missouri. This was in the nature of concession; the Colonel did n't want any trouble with his neighbors. As introductory, it may be said in a broad way that he is accessible and hospitable; that his friends have indeed found a welcome at his hand, and if foes have not always found a grave, it is not because they did not deserve it. Of course, here and there, at long intervals, a just exception might be found, but on the whole, neighbor, on the whole!

Daniel Read Anthony is descended from Quaker stock. This accounts for his being a non-combatant; for the soft, even tenor of his life. By this inherited quality it is he glides into the man who disagrees with him in a mild and healing way truly Anthonese. 'T was ever thus with Daniel. From his youth up his ways have been ways of pleasantness and all his paths peace. For instance, if a division is called on any of the great questions now agitating the country—the 16 to 1 silver ratio; was Dr. Fraker a woman? as between Japs and Pig tails, which?—he would avoid vexatious disputation, nobly advance and offer to sacrifice himself on the altar of his country by compromising at fifty cents on the dollar, assignee to take one-third of the estate for his share. The Colonel came into the world on the south wind, and all along the way he has tarried in gentle dalliance on the sunny side of the peach-trees. It will throw light on our illustrious theme to consider the Quaker essence briefly: I mind me now of William Penn, who divided his time between the tight little isle and the city of brotherly love. You all remember William, the Quakerest Quaker that ever quaked. He came over to introduce the drab fashions to the red man, and, incidentally, to study real estate values. He brought along a new version of the ten commandments, revised and amended for his own particular guidance, and some new adaptations of truth suited to all possible contingencies likely to arise in the course of business in the new world. William despised fire-arms. He would n t drive the red man from his ancient heritage at the point of the bayonet, not he. William was a strategist and knew a thing or two much more valuable to him than dynamite and gunpowder. In a word, he cocked his new version on Red Jacket; that is to say, William traded with Lo; he swapped things with him; he traded beads and pewter beer-mugs and calico handkerchiefs for farms, the good man' And the first thing that Lo knew, he was out of house and home, and looking up a new place to squat. Lo kicked at being turned down in this fashion, but William pulled the record on him, and showed him where he had made his mark, and how, when he had once made a dicker with the pale-face in a drab coat, and "shook," it was a go. This is the way the Quakers got an early and strong cinch on all the virtues, and so have avoided doing wrong, scorning always to imbrue their hands in the blood of their fellow-man, and never would fight for a 'nigger,'' but just slipped him under the wood pile and looked meek and harmless and a little surprised when the owner came along, and

——4

him at the gate with subdued joy, took him into the house, set up
a good dinner, and invited him to call again some time. And when
Kansas began to " bleed at every pore," or words to that effect, and to
cry for help, the Quaker would n't fight, nor nothin' o' that kind, but the
dear old saint, provident in everything, did n't fool away any time. He
engaged vigorously in missionary work among the heathen in Kansas,
and kept the freight agents busy making out bills of lading for cases
marked " books." The work was contagious—mighty ketchen—and
the Quakers of the Penn-Yan city of Penna vied with the Friends of
the staid old commonwealth of Massachusetts in the good work. They
fired the Yankee heart, and the New England clergy, and, in fact,
all the folks in that section of the country—the professional non-com-
batants—the good, the true, the beau—, the die-first fellers, who were
forninst war and all rumors thereof, who favored circumventing the
pro-slavery crowd in Kansas by moral suasion and packed it in those
peculiar, strong, oblong cases marked " books." The Quaker dispen-
sation of literature and method of conversion took like a twelve-dollar
pension, and Preston B. Plumb and the boys met the "books " at the
landing at Nebraska City and placed them where they would do the
most good. Kansas owes a debt of gratitude to the Quakers, and we
don't deny it. The Quakers sent the "books " and Brown of Osawatomie and Jim Lane acted as colporteurs, and made a canvass that
will be remembered down to the wreck of matter and the crash of
worlds.

Having said this much by way of explanation, it must be plain to
every honest man how Leavenworth came into possession of Dan
Anthony. The town during his three-years absence had had trouble
enough, and wished now, in this year of grace 1857, to grow a crop
of poppies and heart's-ease, and invited the young prince of peace at
Rochester to come on.

I always doubted the Quaker antecedents of old John Brown
until I tabulated the incidents of his midnight visitation along the vale
of Osawatomie with his newly ground sword. Not finding the pass-
over blotches on the cabin door-posts up to Quaker grade, the pig-
sticking began; and the trophies were found, as Deputy Beddow, who
accompanied the troops, says, hanging by the heels, and some by one
hand, blackened and ghastly corpses, rotting in the sun !

Old Osawatomie B. made an awkward statement to John Sherman
and his committee concerning this night's work, but on the high moral

plane of the Society of Friends the particulars of this butchery were received with that unruffled calm and resignation so vital to the peace and quiet of the sect.

Col. Dan ran up against a cross-roads sign-post in 1854, the index finger pointing westward, and he took the first train for Kansas. He did not remain long, however, he merely opened the door and looked in. Kansas, in the blessed year aforesaid, was a place where everybody assumed the right to vote. The Colonel, then a young man, in a Kossuth hat and a cut away, the fashion in vogue, shared the universal desire and went up the plank at the old Shawnee House, opposite the site of the Planter's, with a yellow ballot in his hand—the color adroitly adopted to identify the free-state voter without reading the face of his ticket—to vote for delegate to Congress. Fifty disciples of the glorious Democracy of Platte County surrounded the polls, puking tobacco juice and exhaling the aroma of spiritus fermenti, who saluted the late arrival as an "Emigrant Aid Pauper." The sinister glances and protruding chins of the loud-smelling gentry cooled the Colonel s ardor, and with a deep courtesy and that shrinking modesty peculiar to the blood, the suave Quaker backed out and retired. Almost any poor devil north of the classic Waukarusa in 1854 would have done likewise.

Now, we confess, the Colonel was at a loss in this instance; but as a rule, the Friend is sociable, a good mixer, welcome among the boys, wouldn't do anything bad, and always has his weather eye out about election time. Down on the tranquil Waukarusa, in the fifties, the Quaker made good his ancient reputation for being up to date in the exercise of his constitutional right as a free American citizen on election day. As the sun shone out blandly, "Old Broadbrim" not unlike him in genial warmth and jocund smiles, came up and cast a ballot for himself and four others, as he explained to the court in 1855, by proxy, for absent friends. And, bless his dear old heart, he was so serene and open and composed about it—so appealing in his frankness, as much as to say: "Gentlemen, upon your honor, am I not quite right about this?" "In pursuance of the sacred charter of our liberties I deposit my ballot, and these four absent friends of mine they cannot come, as this honorable court will readily allow, for one hath married a wife and must needs pay his devotions, and another hath sold a yoke of oxen and must deliver them, and still another went with the stranger a mile and hath been compelled to go with him twain, and—" the dear old saint stood there, facing the majesty of the law, so placid, of such comfortable girth and ruddy jowl, such benign and sincere aspect, that the just judge, nonplussed, broken by such transparent, child-like innocence, bowed the old gentleman out with profuse apologies, saying that " precedents were lame at best ; that the motive was the chief thing."

In great kindness and with the most benevolent intention we have asked the reader to consider the doctrine of atavism—reversion to the traits of ancestors. It runs in the blood, as witness the scene at the polls in 1858, where Payne and Dunn with drawn revolvers, led the attack on the ballot-box and carried it off, trampling Wetherell, the clerk, under foot, and would have brained him with their favorite tomahawk, the hatchet, but for Brown and the gallant Colonel, who went to the rescue, not to shed blood, messieurs, even in defense of the freeman's rights—not so; the side-arms which they kept well in hand were not positive instruments *de guerre*, but suggestions, and must be historically considered as such.

And that little comedy of errors between Thurston and Anthony ---how could a bit of chiaroscuro like that be set up as an extravagance and a departure on the Colonel's part from the ancient faith of his fathers ? By no means, sweet friends ! Nobody was particularly hurt ; a '54 caliber ball chipped Mr. Douglas's ear, to be sure, and the honorable Mr. Thurston, in a wild attempt to disfigure the moon which had not yet appeared, gave our distinguished and newly-elected Senator Baker a slight inconvenience, but I appeal to any and all of the crack shots of the Leavenworth Gun Club to say whether other than editorial compliment and the usual and time-honored exchange of Leavenworth street civilities can be charged. Certainly not; the marksmanship precludes malice ; the clergy unite upon this view ; the members of the most illustrious bar in the State sanction and defend it ; our venerable city fathers say it's so ; the very able president of this learned body of legislators, summing up, says : "We have examined the ordinances and searched our voluminous precedents for a generation back and find nothing to the contrary. What would gentlemen have ? Is Harlequin to be disowned in his own town ? Let us be reasonable. Here come the querulous with their disputatious babblings, insisting on the loss of life, infractions of the laws, severed friendships, and the general disquiet in 1861. These importunate gainsayers are unfortunate in their selection of dates. 1861 was an uncomfortable year for a great many people. Those of our fellow-citizens who were born in the wrong quarter of the moon, when the sign was n't right having succeeded by the law of entail to the weakness of being too flip, were often surprised by the awkward situations in which they found themselves. They ran up against a stone wall, so to speak. Gentlemen in the discharge of the editorial function were especially liable in 1861 to make remarks on the printed page, the which, in more liberal epochs would be received with positive favor, but in the changed conditions of the Anthony régime, with a sword in the sky, worked like a little earthquake, began the tongues of forked flame breaking through the fissures.

It was all his fault, the poor man! if he had remained on the level, under the conditions of the usual Leavenworth street pistol practice, the ball would have passed over him, harmless, or struck some other man; but he would n't do that; he ran obstinately up the stairway, and was bound if he persisted to come within range of a gun looking upward at an angle of 45 degrees, which he did, at the top of the ascent. Impartial public opinion exonerated the Colonel and must of necessity do so. The most obtuse can see at a glance that the Colonel acted without malice in this affair. His conduct and bearing from first to last was non-committal, as usual, forbearing and Quakerese. As the witnesses testify, he laid down on the lounge in his office and cried; — convincing proof of his innocence, and of the truth of the terms of his biography, written by himself that his Quaker ancestor was "a constant attendant of the Baptist Church," and that an honored member of the family has "devoted more than one fortune to the cause of the moral social, and political elevation of the women of America." Above all things, beloved, let us assume the airs of the "nasty rich," whether we have the "stuff" or not.

But we protest, gentlemen, against the further pursuit of the matter in hand. We have established our case, vindicated the truth of history, and the verdict is ours. Mere innuendo; vague and indefinite charges, involving fists, canes, cow-hides, and saliva, legs, wind, flexures and postures and chairs, dissolving views of the gallant Colonel and "Yaller Tom," and the Red Legs and what not, -all the fistecic fights, big and little, free and circumscribed, which illumine the scribe's fantastic career, these trivial things cannot be admitted as evidence to impeach a fact well known to all, that the Quaker is of that salt of the earth, which has lost the least savour of any of the

absurd sects into which we find ourselves cut up; that while they
have all along protested earnestly against a row of any kind, from a
dog-fight to Gettysburg, the logic of events by which they are influenced and from which they cannot escape, like an atom of water in
some " vast river of unfailing source," in whose destiny they are irrev-
ocably involved and from which they cannot disengage themselves—
the logic of events has forced them to take a hand; and it must be
added to their credit, that they have enjoyed it and wrought nobly for
the Truth and for the advancement of civilization for centuries. Their
sons fought with the foremost and died the death of heroes in all the
battles for the Union, and we have used the career of Col. Daniel Read
Anthony, for whom we have a sincere and hearty respect, to illustrate
our claim that the Quaker is "chock" full of human nature and ain't
going to roll over on his back, and take it when he is kicked, like a
'possum, any oftener than other people. In fine, they follow the Mas-
ter, who would turn the reverse cheek for the second rebuke, if the
facts warranted that course. But right here: let us not deceive ourselves; we do not believe He went among the grasping and insolent
money-changers with a wisp of straw in His hand, crying " Sho ! sho!"
and that the scowling Shylocks fled before Him like sheep; but that
He grasped the thonged lash of the lictor, and when the hook-nosed
misers gnashed their teeth upon Him, He came down upon their
cringing backs with the cuts of the whipping-post, doubly meant ! O,
no ! the corrupt, claw-fingered usurers did not go from the Temple for
the asking, no more than they do to-day ! They went under the scourge
of Him who pointed significantly to the sword when He wanted to
interpret His mission in its profoundest meaning.

We have used the career of Colonel Anthony to illustrate our
contention, that the Quaker feels the force of the great Exemplar's
practice as well as His teaching. What orator stands up nowadays
and visits upon his enemies such scathing denunciations as Christ
flung into the faces of the Pharisees of His day? And do we expect
peace or war from such a course of action? Peace ultimately, but war
as a means to an end.

Leavenworth in 1857 had a population of 4,000. Lots on the
levee were held at $10,000; on Fourth and Fifth streets the price was
$2,000, and along the hills westward the price asked was $1,200.
Prices were advancing; money plentiful; speculation rife. One lot,
that cost $8 at the opening of the spring trade, sold for $2,200 in mid-

summer. Three miles out land sold at $100 per acre, and when platted into lots, at $100 each. The Planter's House had been opened for business in the fall of 1856, and this famous, old time hostelry—now in course of rejuvenation—was overflowing with the incoming tide of fortune seekers.

Leavenworth was justly considered to have decided advantages over the other river towns. It lay contiguous to the Fort. Cincinnati, St. Louis, Chicago, Detroit, and San Francisco had all started as adjuncts to military reservations. The parallel was full of promise, and was accepted as proof, sound as Holy Writ.

Later on, at the close of the war, in 1865, Leavenworth looked more like a great city than any other point between St. Louis and San Francisco. She had three railroads, three daily papers, gas, brick blocks, and the air of a metropolis. There were saloons galore, famous restaurants, and great game, in the lair of the "tiger." The political atmosphere had cleared up after the prolonged and devastating storm of Civil War. The fierce hates and savagery of a decade were exhausted, and many of the leaders in the strife, on both sides, rested in bloody graves. The despicable abolitionist had triumphed at last, and smiled across the street at the discomfited, defeated, and impoverished slaveholder. Most glorious of all, the Union had been saved, and the Republic took on new life and strength, and a securer destiny. Meanwhile the Leavenworth real estate broker leaned over the bar at the Planter's, his ample shirt front lit up by a stone of the first water, and gravely assured his *vis-a-vis* that New York might, possibly, exceed Leavenworth in population for a few years!

St. Joseph, Leavenworth, and Kansas City were the three rivertown rivals, all less than seventy miles apart, and in the year 1865 Kansas City had 11,000 population, St. Joseph 18,000, and Leavenworth 22,000. Now, in this year of grace 1895, close after an interval of thirty years, the equation stands: Leavenworth, 25,000; St. Joseph, 50,000, Kansas City, 150,000. The two Kansas Cities and environs contain 200,000 people. The municipal problem as affected by the military garrison has not met expectations in this instance, but it is too early to give a definite answer as to the final outcome. This much can at least be said with confidence Leavenworth is and ever will be one among the first towns in the Missouri Valley, and beyond all comparison the very first as a desirable place for residence The city is unique among our Western centers of population and progress attractions peculiar to itself, which will grow in importance rather than diminish. She is superior to most of the river towns in manufacturing resources, but as a summer resort, national pleasure ground, and place of residence, she is *par excellence*. A word of admonition, however, is applicable at this point. As a cash investment she should begin at once to enlarge her park attractions; to erect a Chautauqua pavilion, and engage in a summer round of pleasure, which would bring hither, daily, through the season, thousands of visitors, singly, and in groups, and by full train excursions. The new Leavenworth Hotel is right in line with these proposed advances, and the citizens should go forward as one man to the attainment of a higher municipal destiny.

By voting an issue of bonds to run for a long term of years, at a low rate of interest, the city could open up a park on Pilot Knob, to include the beautiful Walnut Grove at the foot of the mountain, on the east. This bold promontory could be made, at small comparative expense, one of the noblest parks in the world. Few cities in the West have such a hill as that close at hand to embellish. The views from the summit are lovely beyond description; and there is a natural growth of forest, and an open space of some ten acres under cultivation, which could be sown to sward and space reserved for games.

The reservoir there is an attraction rather than otherwise. Leavenworth is naturally beautiful for residence, and the expenditure of one million dollars in opening up a magnificent park on Pilot Knob, the valley, including Fort Leavenworth and the National Home, would become irresistible to visitors, and the population of the city would double in less than ten years.

The city possesses substantial backing in other natural resources: in the best and cheapest coal for the furnace, mined at our very doors; in the best fire clays for brick and tile, and in quarries of the best building stone, of easy access. The indications are good for natural gas and coal oil, and discoveries of this kind will some day reward the searcher, beyond doubt. Salt-water baths from natural wells are among the useful features of the town. The city has an abundant water supply, a complete and ample gas plant, an extended trolley system of inter-communication, connecting the most thickly populated districts with Fort Leavenworth and the National Home, and the hotel accommodations will soon rank with the best in the country. The city has a long-established and extensive wholesale trade; her milling and manfacturing plants are notable examples of modern progress and development, and a stove foundry, the third largest in the United States, gives direction to her ambition in the line of home products.

Her glory lies in following the cue providentially given her as a Mecca for the patriotic visitor, and in her super-eminence as a place of residence. Let her, therefore, open up one of the notable public parks of the nation on Pilot Knob, and adorn it and the city with public statues to her martyr heroes. What is required of the city, in a word, is to confess her inventory, covet the best gifts, negotiate a loan, and take her rightful place as an enterprising manufacturing town and chiefest pleasure resort in the Missouri Valley.

Pilot Knob is historic ground. In the dim past the Indian on the war path took his bearings from this projecting hill-top, where he had built a mound of loose stones to guide him by day and from whence a beacon of flame gave him a signal by night. Here the early martyrs to the free-state cause were buried, and as a place of sepulture it was known as Mount Aurora. It ceased to be used as a cemetery when the city placed the enclosed reservoir there, and there is nothing left of the burial plot but the potter's field.

"JAMES H. LANE,

"GENERAL COMMANDING FIRST BRIGADE KANSAS VOLUNTEERS.'

"To all who shall see these presents, greeting."

On yesterday I walked westward along Logan Avenue, following the south line of the Reservation to the Government Farm, the scene of the death of Jim Lane.

What husks are these?

There on a knoll, back from the road, behind a group of trees, now ragged and leafless in the mid-winter suspense stands the old weather beaten farm house of vertical boards, battened, with its row of little three-pane transom windows running under the eave of the upper half story. Across the road, well back, stands an ample barn of forlorn visage, a fit companion-piece in age and storm beaten decrepitude to the cheap wooden structures opposite. Desolate, mean and common.

the meagre group of buildings, one of them untenanted, its window-less eyes staring and pleading for a postponement of the last gasp.

In this land of humble beginnings, large hopes, and great achieve-ment, a senator of the United States might easily have been born in such a house as that, but by what untoward circumstance could one have died there! Ample compensations abound, however. Beautiful as the Vale of Cashmere is the valley where he died, and the encircling hills, covered with forest, rise like a bulwark, even as the mountains lie round about the ancient city of David. Northward, across the billowy pasture-lands, now brown and sere, extending along and out from a grove of oaks, gray and sombre, shines white the stone wall enclosing the National Cemetery; and over and beyond, on the high background, through an opening in the forest, we catch a glimpse of Sheridan's Drive, following the crest of the wooded hills, and half revealed through the leafless trees to the east and north is a row of officers' cottages. In the open front stands a handsome chapel, its spire like a stout dagger against the sky, and out of the depths of the elm-shaded grounds farther away rise venerable barracks and the massive stone and brick walls of ancient and modern garrison build-ings, flanked by still more elegant cottages.

Mr. James H. Beddow, Deputy U. S. Marshal, and his family, now occupy the Farm-house, and dispense a quiet but generous hos-pitality there; the interior being home-like and comfortable, quite in contrast with its neglected exterior.

The Deputy is a veteran of forty-nine years' continuous service with "L'oncle Sam," and in age ranks Fort Leavenworth by a twelve-month, having been born in 1826. Remarkably erect, rugged, and active is this old-time dragoon of the regular service, now in his sixty-eighth year, and he mounts the historic mule with as much ease, apparently, as when he carried dispatches to Major Sedgewick, whose command was reported to have perished when Captain Sam Walker, down on the Waukarusa, literally "fired" Col. Titus, of Florida, out of house and fort by running a load of hay against the blind side of his fortress, and setting a match to it.

On this mild, sunny, midwinter day the Deputy mounted the mule famous in local annals and kindly volunteered to act as guide along the dim, unused, private road which leads from the Government Farm-house northward, over the rolling pasture-lands, past the Cemetery, to the Garrison. Along this road, eight and twenty years ago, Jim

Lane took his last ride The rustic bridges which once spanned the gulches have rotted down and the stone abutments fallen in The unrelenting years, how easily they blind the trail and efface the footprints of our brief and uncertain journey upon the earth '

At a stone's cast from the southeast corner of the Cemetery-wall once ran a partition fence, with a gateway at the point where the road passed through. Here, in the evening of July 1, 1866, on this spot, returning from dress parade at the Garrison, the Government ambulance, containing the senator and his brother-in-law's family, which at that time occupied the Government Farm-house, halted, Lane himself got down and opened the gate, and, as the vehicle passed through, he dropped behind, and with the word "good-bye," placed the muzzle of a pistol in his mouth and fired, the ball passing out at the top of the skull and through his hat The breathing but unconscious man was driven to the Farm-house, where he lingered nine full days and died, without sign, the death of the suicide. Col. D. R. Anthony says that, on visiting him, as he lay on the couch, the dying man made slight signs, and the family thought he recognized his friend, but this seemed incredible for one of even Gen Lane's extraordinary vitality.

To sum up after the fact, we are prone to believe that Lane was a man who, at birth, by "first intention," as the surgeons say, was endowed with that peculiar nervous temperament which, under favoring conditions, would solve the riddle of life by turning upon himself and delivering a fatal stroke. In other words, it does not seem unnatural that this distraught, highly sublimated nature, which ever in its most passionate moments seemed to cross the sane boundary line— it does not seem out of keeping with itself that it should go out in eclipse.

And we believe this to be a sufficient answer to the malicious glee with which his enemies have attempted to becloud a life singularly audacious, wary, and forceful— a career marked by honorable services in the Mexican War, followed by incessant political turbulence and office-holding in Indiana, partisan activity in Kansas in the late fifties, and this again by the chaos, rivalries, savageries, and corruption of civil war And more, the envious and disgruntled may keep on wagging their empty pates and looking preternaturally wise Jim Lane, with all his faults, and we are not blind to any of them, was of the stuff of which heroes are made, and his name and influence in the cause of Free Kansas will live as a popular idol in spite of detraction which has already exhausted itself in a vain effort to dishonor and cloud his memory.

But to return for a moment to the tragedy at the pasture gate.
Is the inference far-fetched that the mind which, as a sensitized plate,
takes on a myriad delicate, almost unconscious, and rapidly succeeding
impressions from nature and all outward objects, received in this
instance the fatal suggestion to end all here and at once from the sweet
and peaceful picture of the cemetery close at hand, upon which his
eyes must have rested as upon the last scene of earth.

> " Here warmly through the fleeting years
>   The summer sun has shone,
> Some winged guest has made its nest
> And tender flowers have grown."

There has never appeared in our national history a more interesting personality than Jim Lane. He was essentially a Western character, and fitted perfectly into his environment in Kansas during the
fifties. There was a providence and a purpose, as we believe there is
something definite in intent and direction in the life of every man—
that went about in the ancient and half bald seal-skin coat and calf-
skin vest. Indeed he was not arrayed like the lily, nor did he come
up as a flower; but rather like a root out of dry ground, typically lean,
and without comeliness; rough and ready in style; not prepossessing
in manners nor appearance; but something of a Lothario, and esteemed
himself dangerous when he met the Sylphide! Tall—more attenuated
than John J. Ingalls—which, on the face of it, appears a preposterous
absurdity. A good figure with which to try conclusions under the
rules of the code, for at a full front there was little to shoot at, and
turned edgewise nothing. The advantages of such a figure under the
conditions alluded to can be better appreciated when we recall Gen.
Jackson's duel with young Dickenson, the best pistol shot of his time
in the South. Jackson, who was himself a good shot and a man of
iron nerve, took no chances at this meeting, and saved his life in the
only possible way left open to him—by cool dishonesty! He appeared
on the field in a loose-fitting but closely buttoned alpaca duster, with
which, by crooking his body imperceptibly, and by introducing another
deception—setting the buttons of his coat an inch out of line—his
enemy was deceived as to the precise line of the heart, and although
he gave "Old Hickory" a wound which he afterward confessed never
healed, and which finally caused his death, was considered as good as
a miss at the time. To conclude this digression, Jackson withheld
his fire, and gave his antagonist a mortal wound, saying that he would

have killed Dickenson even with a ball through his own brain—the
hard headed old scamp'

A plain, beardless face was Lane's—a towering, full forehead, the
whole lit up with eyes that had the glint of genius. In figure and
aspect much like Patrick Henry, but more nearly like him as an orator
than any man who has held a crowd as in the hollow of his hand since
1776. They were unlike, as one star differeth from another star in
glory, in this, that Lane was the incarnation of restless energy and
perseverance, lithe and wiry in muscular frame, capable of great endur
ance, wearing out other men in the saddle.

Always at high tension, the rapidity of his mental processes was
such that he seemed to see the end from the beginning at a glance
while others considered the terms of a proposition, he had already
solved it. His conclusions were intuitions or inspirations expressed,
as on the platform, in oral pictures which his auditors recognized as
true to life and truth. By a single stroke of dramatic speech the crowd
were startled, amused, convinced, aroused to action. In the mixed
assemblages that pressed to hear him on the streets of Leavenworth
and elsewhere on the border there were vicious men who wanted to
kill him ; but they only scowled and listened, for all men, whether
they agreed with him or not, were irresistibly drawn to hear him talk.

Like Patrick Henry, passionate, vehement, intense, unlettered,
an oratorical acrobat, now at the top of the pyramid exultingly sounding the trumpet note of victory, or winding the bugle call to arms, or
descending upon his enemies, like Lucifer from heaven, in a thunder
bolt of wrath' Aflame, his shafts sped afar like arrows of light from
the quiver of the rising King of Day Was there an enemy to punish
he was quenched in his blood-curdling aspirate ' What heights, what
depths were Lane's ' At a bound, bathed in the blending tints and
unspeakable glories of the Delectable Mountains, or lost in the black-
ness of

"The night's plutonian shore'"

A soldier and an orator, his successes were remarkable, but what
transcendent possibilities seemed within a grasp palsied by fatal limita-
tions. Like Stephen A. Douglas, Jim Lane was as blind as the fish
of the Mammoth Cave to the moral aspects of any question slavers
withal; and, like his great contemporary, he was a constant, and to a
degree successful intriguer for Number One ; but to what complexion
did it all come at last? To this, for the ' Little Giant," that he lived

to witness the complete triumph of his incomparable rival, and to hold his hat at his inauguration; and as for Lane—but let us drop the curtain, and proceed to the second act.

Books have been written to damn Jim Lane; and what is the front and burden of his offending? That he was trained in the pro-slavery school and changed tardily, never, down to his last hour, being able to overcome his early prejudices against a "nigger." The first Governor of the State of Kansas, for instance, has consigned Lane to the furnace of purification because he took his cue from the logic of events, along with John A. Logan, John A. Dix, Stephen A. Douglas, Edwin M. Stanton, and a host of others, whom Robinson would exonorate because they were without the Mt. Oread pale of personal rivalry and prejudice.

In what respect were these more noble than Lane? Did they make any greater personal sacrifices for the Union? Ah! my countrymen; prithee, forgive! Thy slave hath forgotten the heroes of a glorious past! I mind me now what time the guns of Sumter summoned the nation to long and bloody war, how Wendell Phillips, Henry Ward Beecher, and their retainers, like Robinson, hatless and bootless, rushed to the front with their ground swords in their teeth, buckling on their scabbards as they ran. Forgive me, friends, this error of mistaking Lane for Robinson—the chief captain of the Union hosts. I confess before the world that in this, to use the language of Uncle Remus, "I dropped my molasses jug."

Here and there, too, the voice of the maligner is heard, questioning Lane's courage. The father of this lie was Quantrell, the groveling scoundrel, who, with sword and torch, stole upon the sleeping town by night to make havoc among women and children. Robinson, a political perfectionist, wrote a book to aid and abet the Quantrell libel, and tries to prove it by Henry W. Halleck and Tom Ewing. Here is a brace of military heroes. Ewing achieved this distinction by the accident of having a brother-in-law who was a soldier in fact, and as for Halleck, he was the most conspicuous and incomparable ass in the long list of dismal failures in the field during the Civil War. He had made some money in California, and, as a part of the by-play of his mighty mind, indulged himself the recreation and divertisement of writing a book on the science of war, in which, in his own fatherly view, was concentered the wisdom of the ages.

In the days of sinning without light or knowledge, immediately following the guns of Sumter, when the corporals and lieutenants of yesterday were the colonels and brigadiers of to day, and the small-bore captains of to-day the major-generals of to-morrow, a plum of the larger size fell to the lot of Henry W.

Nor did his waist measurement fall short on account of it Forthwith he snatched his "grip," and, with a particularly severe and war like frown on his military brow, came east to see what was up. He had knowledge, whilst on the Pacific coast, among other things, of an impecunious and somewhat dissipated, though personally pure and honorable, captain in Uncle Sam's service, who had taken the precaution against dismissal to resign his commission and to precede him to St. Louis, where he was engaged in the arduous duty of trying to support a young and growing family. Roosting high, his two stars nghtter, Henry W. was wont to regard the unfortunate captain, so far as he gave him any thought at all, as an altogether contemptible and worthless person, and was much surprised to hear that he had tendered anew his services to the Government, and had already entered upon the second and last chapter of his military experience.

The great major-general from San Francisco—San Francisco' the glamour of her early days was still potent, and affected the imaginations of men San Francisco, still euphemistic, as lying at the Golden Gate—seemed to add much to the greatness and largeness and mystery of Henry W., who took quarters in St. Louis, establishing himself and his retinue in a mansion of many apartments, and with the usual toggery of guards and flunkies and salaams.

Abreast of all this the poor captain aforesaid borrowed money to get a suit of blue clothing, quietly buckled on his sword and took the field; and all the world knows what happened and how it came to pass.

Henry W., backed by an army of more than a hundred thousand men—veterans of Island No 10, Donelson, and Shiloh—rewarded the devotion of his troops, through his nerveless timidity, with the emptiness, barrenness, and military littleness of the campaign against Corinth During the thirty days of this twenty-mile advance Halleck was invisible to his troops, as much of a myth as the Caliph of Bagdad. We never saw him riding along the outposts alone, like Grant at Mission Ridge, who personally knew every foot of the ground he was to fight over, and who was not averse to the humorous phases of the situation, and could sit on his horse and talk to the rebel picket across the creek! O, he was a dear old man, Grant was '

Fortune favored Henry W., nevertheless, and he hied him to Washington in a palace car.

The silent captain of cordwood memory quietly went to Washington also, by a circuitous route, the names of the stations being Belmont, Henry, Donelson, Shiloh, Vicksburg, Mission Ridge, The Wilderness, Appomattox.

The one began with a bank account and a major-general's commission, and ended where he began, his escutcheon an absolute blank. The other rose out of deepest poverty and the command of a regiment, to be the first soldier of modern times; a ruler outranking kings; called to temporary sovereignty by the will of a free people, in a Republic of imperial domain, incalculable wealth, unapproachable in military power—not in the strength of her standing armies, but in her matchless faith in herself, interpreted as the will of God!

It was in the early days at St. Louis, when Henry W. Halleck, domiciled in the clouds as commander of the department, that Dr. Robinson sought the General's aid to crush Jim Lane. He might as well have tried to put out the sun with a squirt-gun, for as a current maxim common to everybody, there was more horse-sense in one hour of Jim Lane's active brain than filtered through the brain of Halleck during the whole war.

As fertile and resourceful in political intrigue as Machiavelli or old Talleyrand, his was real genius in the advancement of things essential to his personal glory or profit. A Cæsarian ambition indeed, without which he would be less than man. As a bold rider he could endure with the Apache, the Cossack, or the Tartar. His thighs no larger than the ankles of some men, he wrapped those withe-like legs under his horse with a cinch of his own, and clung to his saddle like a wraith. At the halting-place he would say to his boys, "Now give me twenty minutes for a nap," and he would fling himself at full length on the ground, bury his face in his arms, and sleep like a child, rising as fresh betimes as though he had slept for hours.

Few of our public men, of the last generation, possessed Lane's talents for both the field and the council chamber, but this double equipment in him was a source of weakness, for, the temptation in both directions being equally strong, he was at constant war with himself, and he no sooner felt success within his grasp in one direction than he abandoned the pursuit for fear of losing something in the other, and so his reward was less than if he had given himself unre-

servedly to either.   His rivals and foes in political council had reason
to remember him, for he was not the least successful aspirant of his
day, but it always appeared to the best judges of the time easily possible for Jim Lane to have become a great leader of cavalry.   Beyond
question, he had many of the choicest gifts of the true son of Mars.
Daring, yet wary ; intrepid and impetuous, yet coldly calculating.   But
above all, he could inspire his men as no other could do, and all things
seemed possible to him as a soldier.

 " He is a very persistent fellow," said Abraham Lincoln in 1863 ;
" he is at my door every morning."   Lane was conscious of his ability
to do worthy things in the field, but was loth to give up both honors
and fame in the Senate, and so fell short altogether.

We cannot close this desultory and imperfect sketch of a great
partisan leader without a passing glimpse of him at the head of the free-
-state force before Lecompton, where they had laid siege to the town to
enforce the demand for the release of the free-state prisoners.   The
strong arm of the Government interposed to keep the peace, and as
Col. St. Geo. Cooke rode up to the patriots in the brush on his errand
of intervention and asked H. Miles Moore in a tone of authority for
" the commander of this force," Lane stood under a tree some distance
away, clad in a blue woolen shirt and slouch hat, conveying to his
lieutenant by mental telegraphy and meaning glances his caution to be
non-committal on all leading questions.   The suspense at this moment
was aching with strong desire on the part of the free-state boys to
"knock h— out of Old Shannon and his capital," and on the part of
the Government to exercise the paternal sovereignty to prevent a
fight, although the regulars, divided in sentiment, on general principles
would as soon have a little "scrap " as not.

Bayonets, in a free country, do a good deal of hard thinking on
occasion, and we can't wonder at 'em—and right here we stop long
enough to ask, How long will it be in our dear native country, with
an army largely composed of heterogeneous material, saturated with
the current social ferment and error, before the guns in action will be
turned against us, as the French troops went over to the enemies of
the state in the revolutionary period?   It is now proposed to draw in
strong detachments of the military and quarter them in permanent
posts near the great centers of our population.   Can you guess the
far-reaching portent of all this?

Enough ; to our muttons: There stood Old Bicknell with his battery of one gun—a duplicate of "Old Kickapoo"—crying. "O, just give me one shot at 'em! I've got her loaded to the muzzle, just let her roar once!" Col. Cooke finally succeeded in getting Maj. Moore to point Lane out, with whom it was arranged that the besiegers should retire.

Fun? One day the "boys," as he was wont to call his devoted followers, in hilarious conclave, affected to question the General's modesty. Addressing them from the platform in one of those inimitable speeches, he adverted to this personal characteristic and said, gravely, that on coming to his majority, his dear old mother, deeply concerned for his welfare, anticipating the difficulties he would encounter—the thorny barriers which bar the progress of the ambitious, "Henry," said she, solemnly, "you know that modesty runs in the b'ood; that this trait in your ancestors has, by the law of heredity, come to unwonted perfection in you, and I charge you, Henry, to — Here his voice was lost in the chopping sea of badinage, yells, and laughter, and awaiting the pleasure of the good-natured crowd, he stood like an attenuated Uncle Sam, in affected astonishment.

For good or ill the books are closed against the record of this Knight of the Border, and his name and fame are being rapidly transmuted into a sort of legend like that of Francis Marion, the Swamp Fox of the Carolinas. These men were both a prime necessity to a great cause in the region where they operated, and so long as Truth is justified of her children, the memory of both will be cherished, admired, and praised. The envious who hasten to distort the truth and exaggerate weaknesses, because of conscious inferiority in their attempt to measure up to the subject of this sketch, may indulge their gibes—there are men still living, good and true—veterans of the Kansas fifties—who swear that Jim Lane was the truest man to his friends and to his country that God ever made!

> " Revile him not, the tempter hath
> A snare for all,
> And pitying tears, not scorn or wrath,
> Befit his fall."

The Missouri Pacific Railway—the great southwest system—see page 94.

1,000 VETERANS AT DINNER.

THE NATIONAL HOME.

Visitors to the Western Branch of the National Home, Leavenworth County, Kansas, usually desire to be shown the Ward Memorial building, occupied as headquarters by the officers of the branch. Here a guide may be found who will conduct strangers through the public library and the other places of interest.

A glimpse at the wards in the barracks, with a word of detail as to " how we live," is always acceptable to those who are making their first call.

The dinner hour at 12 M. is the general assembly, which the visitor will wish to take in. If it is on a Wednesday or Sunday, the Home Band, under Prof. Meyrilles, will give four selections, divided between the first and second tables. The dining hall is one of the noblest apartments of its kind in the Union.

The kitchen, superb in its appointments, adjoins at the rear. Delay here from 11:30 to 12 o'clock and see the food dished up and rolled down the center aisle on the wheeled " two-deckers." Tarry till the gong sounds and see 1,000 men pass in and take their seats. There would be lots more fun in it for you if the captain would "hunch" you in the ribs and tell you to "sit down and take suthin'," but don't feel slighted if he seems to forget. You are hungry enough to eat

seven raw turnips, and he knows it and is feeling awful mean about
it but he's doing business for his Uncle with a big U, and you know
how it is yourself, we can get along with almost anybody better than
with our own kin. When you are tired looking at other people raid
the dinner table, fall back on the Home Restaurant, where you will
find a twenty-five-cent spread that will make you feel like staying
around for a week or two. And if there is anything lacking at the
close of the feast, a sort of goneness, as it were, which the pale, pictorial amber might alleviate—but there we go again; Uncle don't
allow it. There are some drawbacks in being a free American citizen,
after all.

The Canteen is open to the veteran, but closed to the citizen.
That is to say, in the Canteen and the Gold Cure our glorious uncle has
provided for both the veteran's temptation and his redemption   So
kind of Uncle Sam! And there are people exploiting themselves over
a condition that has made Keeley a millionaire

Another curious coincidence in connection with the Canteen in
operation at the National Home has long been a matter of public
comment   I refer to the singular concurrence of the regular quar-
terly payment of pensions and the prompt arrival at the Home of two
cars of Anheuser Busch's "best" direct from St. Louis.   In noting this
regularly recurring incident, now for some years looked upon as a part
of the slated order of business in the Home administration, no one has
thought for a moment of construing it as a special provision whereby
the Home treasury might profit by the excesses at the Canteen on and
immediately after pension day   Perish the thought!

Are we not engaged in a great moral reform, and is there any
thing "out of gear," as it were, in the association of Keeley with pretzels?
Our fears are quieted and all doubts put to rest when the chaplain
stands up in his place on the first day of the week and points with
pride to our twin home industries and cries at the top of his voice   "We
are the people!"

And to say the least of it it is peculiar that one should be looked
upon as a public enemy who has the temerity to make a passing comment upon this feature of "Home" life

The young ladies who are with you are ready now for a diversion;
take them over to Lake Jeannette, where you will find elegant shells
at your service for an hour's spin on the water, and good black bass
fishing also

LAKE JEANETTE AND HOSPITAL W. B. N. H. D. V. S.

The immense hospital is near at hand, and the annex for convalescents also, both of which possess a sad interest for the friends of the veterans.

Chief Surgeon D. C. Jones is in charge, with a competent staff of assistant surgeons and an efficient corps of trained nurses.

We hope at no distant day to see the Home grounds and certain reservations at the Fort provided with convenient and elegant pavilions, lavatories, and seats, so that the tired visitor, particularly women and children, may not dread a day's outing at these beautiful grounds.

The bugle is sounding "retreat" under our barrack window. Night and silence have fallen, and a brigade of two thousand men are in their blankets. I always try to go to sleep before the bugle sounds; otherwise it may keep one brooding and sad far into the night. It is the bugle that gives us pause, and over the open grave of the veteran it speaks the same strain of farewell.

The legions of memories its lingering notes recall to newness of life! The remembrance of vast battle-fields, covered with smoke; the swollen figures of the slain; the swift passage of batteries; the sullen boom of distant guns; the exultant shout from thousands of throats, receding down miles of battle-front like lessening thunder! It is the bugle note that speaks loudest to me of the fullness of the past and

the leanness of the present. Then we rode on life's tumultuous, topmost wave; now we are in the trough of the sea, water logged and foundered. Then our faces were glorified by the reflected light of the red shield of Mars; now we sit like stuffed toads and blink the heavy hours away!

I had been away on furlough for a year. On my return I asked 'Mack' about the death of Bob. This poor lad of sixty years belonged to an Indiana battery and in his day had been a shrewd man of the world. He was a near relative of Vinnie Ream, the artist, whose statue of Lincoln stands in the National Pantheon at Washington. "It was a winter's night here in old Ward One," said Mack, "and Bob was very bad, we were up with him the most of the night, and in the morning he was taken to the convalescent barrack for better care. There he sank rapidly and soon died. The burial day was inclement and the regular funeral escort did not turn out, and so Andy and I and a few others went out and saw poor Bob laid away." It is so that these men, who have made the names of Grant and Sherman and Meade and Thomas and Sheridan immortal, recross the ghostly shore and have laid them down where the ancient river rolls

I have always admired the picture of the old American fifer of the Revolution, in the full bloom of his desperate patriotism! Look at him, hatless, as his proud form strides along, his nether jaw drawn down and giving forth the ear-piercing notes of "Yankee Doodle." Patrick Henry's defiant outburst has sunk deep into his soul, and the old man is young again, and depend upon it, he would stand with his well-ground sword and defend the flag of his country against the world! O yes; we laugh at and embrace him with all our heart.

A GHASTLY SACRILEGE.

It is the soldier's choice and his glory to be buried where he fell. What a ghastly sacrilege is this in which ye have been engaged! Let these sleepers rest the awful ages through on the spot where they died. Ye are building lettered memorials on the sacred spot. Why do ye tear their bones from the earth baptized with their blood? But ye have taken away the lords of our battle-fields, and where have ye laid them? Our immortal dead once had hallowed sepulture by powder-grimed hands that loved them well, and on the field of their fame. And now ye come with rude jest, irrelevant banter, and profane touch to disturb their deep repose, and to cart their poor bones away to alien soil, where in rectangular and conventional preciseness the paltry stones rise in meaningless rows! Our children will forever worship on yonder mount of sacrifice; but ye say the National Cemetery is the place to worship. Did not the stones cry out, and was no voice raised against this violation of the gory sepulchres of our kings? This is the cemetery indeed, but yonder is the shrine; here is the landscape gardener and his rod and chain, but yonder is the soil stained with the blood of heroes!

And this is the fitting place! Here nature reigns; here is the tangled grass, the wild flower in its native grace, the strange sweet odors of the wildwood. Here our native songsters wake the morning echoes with their jubilant chorus, and here in piteous plaint they softly breath their vesper hymn. Here lift your cenotaphs; here let your sinuous paths wind; here lie the flower of our youth—true princes of the blood; and here, in the name of Christ our Lord, let them rest "till the night is gone and the shadows flee away"!

Look about you! Seest thou these sentinel pines, these ancient oaks, riven by the thunderbolts of war? these majestic elms, graven deep, and their hearts laid bare by the vengeful wedges of battle?

Here in one awful hour the wrongs of centuries were righted.

And now ye come here in your thoughtless pity to gash again earth's bleeding bosom, and take from her fond embrace the dust which she hath received back to her nourishing heart!

I bless God ye labor in vain! Ye may indeed drag forth these poor bones, but the brave hearts that once beat high at the rising tide of battle, and the fair young faces once lit by the flame of smoking guns, this dear earth hath received them to herself, and the old, old mother mocks at your picks and shovels.

Away with you! In the sight of men and angels ye are accursed! Come not here with your polluting touch, for this is holy ground.

As we tread these solemn heights, out of the sighing wind comes an appealing voice, saying: "It is the will of God; let us rest in peace!"

Hover still over the plains of Marathon, legend says, the ghosts of Hellenic heroes; Miltiades and his group of generals are there, and the voices of the night give forth the shock of wide extended battle! And we doubt not that the spirits of the fallen sons of the Republic revisit the scenes where in mortal strife Truth was made manifest. To this holy of holies the youth of America may come to gird his sword on his thigh, and to swear eternal fealty to the stars that pale not and to the stripes that have waved in triumph on a thousand battle fields!

Divorce, except for heinous crimes, is accursed of God, and this one of the removal of our slain from the spot where they fell, perpetrated by heedless, misguided, and unsanctified authority, is doubly regretful in every thoughtful mind.

After the battle of Mission Ridge and the flight of the rebel army, and following our return from Knoxville, I stood in the late autumn of 1863 upon the battle-field of Chickamauga. The Federal dead were fitly resting where they fell, and on Gen. Thomas's front I marked the position of a rebel battery, the scarred and trampled earth still giving every sign of the harvest of death reaped here! On this spot I picked up the eyelet end of a leather tug of artillery harness, severed by a sabre stroke. The eyelet itself was not the smooth and polished casting such as adorned the Federal harness, but had been patiently beaten out and fashioned on the anvil and rudely but stoutly riveted to the leather, and the small relic had an interest of its own could it have spoken its own history. Here in "one red burial blent" lay an officer and sixteen men of a Louisiana battery, and I challenge earth to show a nobler burial. Here together, "on the field of their fame, fresh and gory these American soldiers—our foes that day—gave proof of their manhood and of the glorious stuff of which American soldiers are made by sealing their claim to the world's admiration with their blood. And palsied be the hand that could break in upon their glorified slumbers, and cart off the kingly sleepers to a cheap and second-hand funeral in alien soil.

What wreck profane hands have made of this altar of American valor in these two and thirty years I know not, but I have a strong suspicion that the desecration has been complete, as of all others.

And say what you will, the misgiving will forever abide that the sleeper beneath is not correctly portrayed by the inscription on the headstone.

In my admiration of these fallen braves I had forgotten that they had ever been our enemies.

What boots that ye cannot name every sleeper in the lowly bed where he was first laid. This ye were not able to do in any event, and so much the less reason for disturbing them.

I, for one—and there are millions like me—wash my hands of this unwonted, untimely, profane resurrection of our dead.

The noblest inscription ever graven in granite to commemorate our illustrious dead, slain in defense of the integrity and honor of the Union, is that significant and solemn declaration :

To the Unknown.

Only the great stone rests not upon the right spot.

Eternal truth, and the immeasurable heritage of the Father's love which he hath bestowed upon his children, as expressed in the ideal love of country, is nobly declared and vindicated in these three words; and I call the youth of my country to witness that if there be any consolation, and inspiration for human hearts in the surrender of life and one's very name to the glory and perpetuity of the Republic, it may be found in these awful words of mystery and sacrifice. Sons and daughters of our dear Columbia, seek ye for proof of the high ideal of patriotic devotion in the heroic age of the Republic? Fling your flowers here, and upon this block of memorial granite hang your wreaths of immortelles.

The ill-trained hirelings were too uncertain in their botched and reckless work of fitting and joining the poor bones broken and splintered by the iron sledges of war. Out of such a jumble as stands

to their charge the poor lads will have trouble in adjusting their artic-
ulated framework when the angel with one foot on land and one on
sea shall sound the general reveille.

I know very well that it would vex me to stand there in the ' dark
offing' with my wings folded and look on at those fellows giving my
skull (on an even trade') for that fellow's femur, and this most excellent
tibia of mine, fit for service, they toss to Tom because he seems to be
short, and for one great toe mislaid they offer me nothing at all,
although there are plenty of square-toed feet to choose from. No, sir'
I could wish they had let me alone. I was doing very well. The boys
gave me the best lodgings they had on the dark and bloody ground,
and the sweet-smelling turf has healed the wounds for which there
was no other earthly balm.

And now these lewd fellows of the baser sort come here to take
me away from the bed fellows once wrapped with me in the wrathful
fires of contending hosts, and to put me—what they can find of me
in strange quarters, pieced out with bits of other folk' And all the
consolation I have is in seeing the giant there, who requited me ill,
compelled to give up the best part of his backbone for the dwarf's
basket of ribs, which make a sorry display and inadequate neath the
chin of the disgruntled Goliath.

Gentlemen, I am ashamed of you for this day's work, and of my
dismantled condition, and salute you with such grace as a soldier with
a disfigured and much mixed identity can command.

SOLDIERS' HOMES IN FOREIGN LANDS

PENSIONERS LEAVING THE INVALIDES.

Before very long it is expected that the Hotel des Invalides—the
gilt dome of which forms such a conspicuous landmark in Paris—will
have ceased to exist, at all events as what may be called the home of
the French Chelsea pensioners. By degrees the number of pensioners
lodged there has diminished until they are a mere handful. It seems
that old soldiers do not care to continue to live in barracks after their
retirement, but that they prefer a pension outside, be it ever so small.
Owing to the decrease in the number of pensioners, a public sale has
been held at the place of furniture and other superfluous articles.

REVIEW OF 1ST BAT. KEELEY LEAGUE AND SECTION "A" 1ST VET. BATTERY, NAT. MIL. HOME, COL. ANDREW J. SMITH, COMMANDING.

Elegant Millinery Goods

J. E. VINCENT HAIR & MILLINERY CO.

The Leading Imported and Domestic Toilet and Complexion Goods.

Theatrical Goods, Grease Paints, General Stage Make-up, Wigs,
Beards, Mustaches, Creppe Hair, Wool and Spirit Gum.

Perfect Fitting Wigs and Toupees Made to Order.

Modern Turkish Baths

J. E. VINCENT HAIR AND MILLINERY CO.,

Some old clothing, belonging to dead and gone pensioners, was also disposed of. Among the kitchen utensils brought to the hammer was a copper saucepan, no longer needed, which was so large that it took six men to carry it to the cart on which it was taken away. A facetious bidder, who asked the auctioneer whether he would put up the pensioner's "wooden head," of which French legend speaks, was informed that unfortunately that interesting object was not included in the catalogue.

CHELSEA HOSPITAL.

The Chelsea Hospital was founded to provide a suitable home for soldiers disabled by wounds or age. It was the first national provision created in England for veteran soldiers as a class. In Ireland, its sister establishment at Kilmainham, in the suburbs of Dublin, was erected about the same time, for the relief of soldiers on the separate Irish Establishment. That hospital still survives as a home for pensioners, selected from those resident in Ireland. It is separately governed on a system similar to that in force in Chelsea.

The standing or Parliamentary Army of England was first raised in the year 1660. From that time, therefore, dates the system of enlisting soldiers into the service of the country as a profession requiring the best parts of their lives, and the consequent obligation on the part of the country to make provision for their general support in old age.

The necessity of a national provision having thus arisen on the creation of a standing army, difficulty in supplying it was felt, owing to the reluctance of Parliament to vote more than the merest pittance for the service of the army, scarcely sufficient for the pay and allowances of the soldier serving. Under these circumstances, to meet the desire of Charles II. to save his old soldiers from indigence, an ingenious minister devised a plan for the erection of a hospital or home without appealing to Parliament for the necessary funds. Sir Stephen Fox, the Paymaster-General of the Forces, who had accumulated a considerable fortune by his financial relations with the soldier, was generous enough to give in return personal assistance towards this end, and clever enough to procure from the Army itself the bulk of the funds, by deductions from pay under certain conditions, by the contribution of a day's pay in the year, and in other ways. The King appealed to the public also for voluntary aid, but the appeals were not very successful.

The accounts are still in existence, and the exact figures shown. The whole of the voluntary contributions did not amount to 20,000*l*. The King gave in addition nearly 7,000*l*., an unapplied balance of secret service money. Chelsea Hospital may therefore be said to have been mainly built by the Army itself, as a home for its veterans. Its lands were purchased in the same way, and increased from the proceeds of legacies. Parliament can claim no ownership over either. As a well-known writer concisely states, " Within the walls of Chelsea Hospital the veteran has indeed nothing to complain of—but why ? Because the establishment is his own, built by his own or his predecessor's money." It is true that the current support of the soldier in the Hospital is voted by Parliament, as the soldier's pay is voted, that support being his deferred pay due to him by right of his contract on enlistment. The Hospital, therefore, is in no sense a charity. The soldier is there in enjoyment of honest independence, earned by long and arduous devotion to his country's service.

There can be no doubt that it was the intention to have a home sufficiently large to accommodate all entitled to admission. And when the foundation-stone was laid in 1682 the estimate of space was fairly formed. By the time, however, of the completion of the building, ten years later, the expectants had grown in number, and when it was opened it was found necessary to give out-pensions to a few whose admission had to be deferred. Thus arose the Chelsea Out-Pensions, and the rapid and continuous increase of the Army soon led to the out-pensioners becoming the larger body, in time dwarfing into insignificance the relative proportion of the in-pensioners, so much so as at the present day to be 160 to 1. This unexpected state of things has altered to some extent the scheme of in-pension, making it now the provision for a selected number from the out-pensioners, the blind, the paralyzed, the decrepit from diseases of various kinds, and the very aged, all unprovided with suitable homes amongst their friends, and for whom any ordinary allowance in money could not serve to provide homes in their individual capacities. Considering that the out-pensioners are now about 55,000 in number, it may be inferred how many fall under this description. About 98 per cent of the sum goes to out-pensioners, the remainder to in-pensioners, the latter numbering 540 at Chelsea and 150 at Kilmainham.

Locally, Chelsea Hospital has obtained the character of other utility by reason of its gardens, which are large and well kept, open to the public on much the same conditions as the larger parks, and from long usage now inalienable to other purposes, though their maintenance is not a charge on Parliamentary funds. They comprise about sixty acres of open space, the greater part of which is accessible freely to the public.

The selection of in-pensioners is made, as already stated, from the body of out-pensioners, and on the principle that those only are admitted who from age or suffering cannot employ their time to their own advantage in civil occupations, and are without suitable homes with their friends or families. The rules for the guidance of the Commissioners in making the selection are issued by the Queen. In-pensioners are removed from the out-pension list, their wants in food and clothing being supplied from the Hospital funds, and a small money allowance in addition for tobacco, etc. The labor required in the Hospital is almost all performed by the in-pensioners themselves, and for this they are paid. One hundred and seventy small plots of garden are assigned to this number of men, from the cultivation of which with flowers and vegetables they earn some money, visitors being willing purchasers. Thus, between employment in light hospital labor and the garden cultivation, a large proportion of in-pensioners earn some money, almost every pensioner who is at all capable of physical exertion. Residence in in-pension, though eagerly sought, is not afterwards enforced, any man being allowed to return to out-pension and quit the Hospital when he pleases, and a few are found to avail themselves of this privilege, for discontent and desire of change are found amongst this class as amongst all others. In almost every instance, however, early application is made for permission to return. A pensioner who makes himself a discomfort to others by much irregularity of any kind is made to revert to out-pension, but stricter discipline is not enforced. In addition to all usual wants in diet, clothing, and housing, a staff of medical men and nurses reside for the care of the sick and feeble, and an infirmary with 100 beds, which are found inadequate for demands. Church services for the three leading religious bodies are provided by the Commissioners, and the chaplains and church visiting organizations encouraged to afford every aid. Friends visit the pensioners without restriction, and the latter move about the neighborhood at will within reasonable hours. Furlough is allowed to those who desire to visit their friends in country places.

The first stone of the Hospital was laid by the King on 17th February, 1681-2. Ten years later the building was ready for occupation, though not completed till 1694. In prints of the day the structure appears just as it now is, without the smallest subsidiary buildings since added for the secretary's office, and, on the opposite side, some officers' quarters, and the large range of infirmary buildings, all of which were built or acquired in the early part of the present century.

The sums expended for land, building, and furnishing in twenty years from 1681 amounted to 157,000*l.*, from which it may be inferred that the main structure cost 130,000*l.*

The appropriation of the several parts of the building to their respective uses seems to have remained unaltered from the first. There are · (*a*) berths for 510 men, all separately enclosed (100 more beds are found in the infirmary); (*b*) great kitchen, in which the whole of the food is prepared, save infirmary diets prepared in the infirmary itself; (*c*) chapel, with seats for 300 pensioners, and pews for the officers; (*d*) great hall, formerly a dining-room, but now a general day-room, the pensioners dining in messes in their wards; (*e*) library, containing 4,000 volumes of books and liberal supply of newspapers and magazines; (*f*) quarters for 13 military officers and for non-commissioned officers and apartments for nurses. A gardener's lodge, an improved laundry, and a model bakery have been erected within recent years. Bread supplied by contract, from one cause or another, never gave satisfaction.

The decadence of Waterloo veterans is almost complete. There were 58 in the Hospital in the year 1870, 36 in the year 1872, 15 in 1876, 11 in 1878, 9 in 1879, none in 1885.

The dietary of 430 pensioners is shown in the following table. The remaining number, say 110, are dieted in the infirmary, according to arrangements ordered by the medical staff to suit their various wants. Meat of best quality only, is contracted for, and full power given to the officers to reject it if inferior

Each man daily Bread, 1 pound, butter, 1 ounce, good cocoa, ¾ of an ounce, good moist sugar, 1 ounce, in the morning, good black tea, ⅛ of an ounce, good moist sugar, ½ of an ounce, in the evening, the best new milk, ⅛ of a pint, imperial

On Sundays and Wednesdays for each man Beef, 13 ounces, potatoes, 1 pound, flour, 5 ounces; best beef suet, 1½ ounces; best washed currents, 1 ounce, rice, ½ an ounce.

Five days per week each man: Mutton, 13 ounces; potatoes, 1 pound; barley, Scotch, ½ an ounce. On Fridays: Cheese, ½ a pound.

Or in lieu of these, when demanded: On Sundays for each man: Beef, 13 ounces; potatoes, 1 pound; rice, 4½ ounces; suet, ½ an ounce; sugar, 1¼ ounces; milk, ¾ of a pint, imperial; or, beef, 13 ounces; potatoes, 8 ounces; cabbage or other vegetable, 1 pound.

On Wednesdays for each man: Bacon, 10 ounces; potatoes, 8 ounces; cabbage or other vegetable, 1 pound.

Strangers usually desire to see the chapel and hall, the wards, the public monuments, and the gardens.

The chapel and great hall are of the same size, each 108 feet long and 37 feet wide.   The ceiling of the former being coved and of the latter flat, the proportions of the apartments appear different.   Both chapel and hall are hung with flags, taken from the enemy in war, and for the most part transferred here from other places in the year 1835 by King William IV.   Of those in the hall scarcely more than the poles survive, but those in the chapel are in a fair state of preservation. In addition to the flags, the chapel contains many eagles taken from the French Army.   The following flags, etc., may be mentioned as fairly preserved and identified:

American flag, 68th Regiment, *James City*, *Light Infantry*.   An Eagle, on white ground, with stars and the scroll "E Pluribus Unum." On the reverse, red stripes and cap of Liberty and "Virginia" on a blue band.   Captured at Bladensburg by the 85th Regiment in 1814.

American cavalry flag, captured by same regiment at same place. An eagle on blue ground.   1*st Har...., Light Dragoons.*   "*Touch Me Not*" on scroll.

American flag.   Eagle on blue ground.   2*d Regiment of Infantry.* Date of capture not known.

No. 26.   Eagle of 62d French Regiment, taken at Salamanca in 1812.

No. 38.   Eagle of 22d French Regiment, taken at same place.

Of these two eagles the following accounts were published:

" Lieutenant Pearce, of the 44th, had the honor of capturing a " French eagle at the glorious battle of Salamanca.   This officer, " attached to the 5th or General Leith's Brigade, was ordered with his " regiment to charge the French Infantry, now thrown into confusion " by the valour of our men.   Seeing the trophy unscrewed from the " staff and in the act of being concealed, he gallantly attacked the

" Frenchmen, from whose hands he wrested it and presented it on the
" field of battle to the General, who requested him to retain it and pre-
" sent it the following morning to Lord Wellington "

(On the 20th May, 1847, this officer called at the Hospital to see
the eagle, for capturing which he obtained his company.)

Eagle and flag of the 45th French Regiment taken by Sergeant
Ewart, Scots Greys, at Waterloo.

Extract from a letter which Sergeant Ewart (afterwards Ensign,
5th Royal Veteran Battalion) wrote to his father relative to the capture of this eagle:

" It was in the first charge about 11 o'clock, I took the eagle from
" the enemy. He and I had a hard contest for it. He thrust for my
" groin, I parried it off and cut him through the head, after which I
" was attacked by one of their Lancers, who threw his lance at me,
" but missed the mark by my throwing it off by my sword at the right
" side; then I cut him from the chin upwards, which went through his
" teeth. Next I was attacked by a foot soldier, who, after firing at me,
" charged me with his bayonet, but he very soon lost the combat, for
" I parried it and cut him down through the head, so that finished the
" contest for the eagle. * * * * * I took the eagle into Brussels
" midst the acclamations of thousands of spectators who saw it "

Extract from the Guide to Captain Siborne's New Waterloo Model

" As the Scots Greys passed through and mingled with the High-
" landers, the enthusiasm of both corps was extraordinary. They
" mutually cheered, 'Scotland forever" as their war-shout The smoke
" in which the head of the French column was enshrouded had not
" cleared away when the Greys dashed into the mass. * * * Within
" that mass, too, was borne the imperial eagle of the 45th Regiment,
" proudly displaying on its banner the names *Jena, Austerlitz, Wag-
" ram,* and *Friedland,* fields in which this regiment had covered itself
" with glory, and acquired the distinguished title of the Invincibles.
" A devoted band encircled the sacred standard, which attracted the
" observation and excited the ambition of a daring and adventurous
" soldier named Ewart, a sergeant of the Greys etc etc '

Eagle and flag of the 105th Regiment, taken by Captain Clark
(Kennedy) and Corporal Stiles of the 1st Royal Dragoons, at Waterloo.
Inscription, "*Jena, Eylau, Echnwil, Ratting, Wagram*' On the reverse,
'L'Empereur Napoleon au 105 Regiment d Infanterie de ligne'

The hall has been the scene of some remarkable events the court martial on the conduct of General Whitelocke; the court of inquiry into the Convention of Cintra; the laying in state of the Duke of Wellington, 10th to 17th November, 1852; the Crimean inquiry, etc. A number of old pensioners, who had served under the Duke, gathered from all parts of the kingdom, followed the body from Chelsea to St. Paul's.

The world had n't laughed since the crucifixion till America was discovered, and Uncle Sam went up against the pewter crowns of Europe in his best suit of stripes and swallow-tail and told the unicorns rampant that they might consider him in the race.

This he did with his characteristic good humor, his famous bell-crowned hat under his arm, dispensing right and left his most gracious compliments, his truly beautiful and profound genuflections. He was so entirely at home, so much at his ease, and through it all there shone so much of that peculiar occidental brusque-nerve, so much of the daring of the Brulé-Sioux brave, that while the mitred Brownies hated, they feared, but would not acknowledge him till he had tied Burgoyne and Cornwallis up by the thumbs, put Packingham to sleep at New Orleans, and sunk their pirate *Alabama* off Cherbourg harbor.

They know us now, and we laugh, and the poor serfs in distant lands, who have not had a good laugh in twenty centuries, laugh now and with us, a big hopeful laugh, at the big fellow across the sea who wears the stripes of his flag in his breeches and the stars thereof in his " westcut," and who don't care a continental for none of them.

Back in 1850 this eagle-beaked old uncle went over to Japan, his genial peach-colored face all aglow with love for his kind, and knocked at the door of the strange little seagirt isle: " Hello! " he cried, in kind old-fashioned greeting ; " hello, little one ! come out into the fresh air and be one of us !" And he thrilled the little yellow chap with that touch of nature we all know about, and lo, what a little encouragement has done ! Yesterday Li Hung Chang, the friend of Gen. Grant and our friend, got into trouble and comes with confidence to our grand old uncle to help him adjust his difficulties with his neighbors. And the Frenchman is onto the situation and solves the riddle by announcing the last advent—America, the seventh of the great European powers.

The past is illustrious with the names of Washington, Adams, and Franklin, the future of my country glorious beyond conception, but as for me, I am satisfied to have lived contemporary with Abraham

1017 Walnut St, Kansas City Mo

Lo In Ca   S Grant, W'   am Tecumseh Sh rm G   H
Th r   and the host of kn wn and unknown her   wh   in u l
n!   ma th supr m   l triumphant stru   f   th U   n
    nd   our   thers.

ONE, TWO, THREE,

AND HOW THEY COME OUT.

When I think of Waterloo three figures step out to view—Wellington, Napoleon, and the Belgic housewife. And it occurs to me to say here that, while some men are building empires, others are engaged in tearing them down, and still others are raising cabbages—all of them labors necessary to the advancement of the race, and no one of them less valuable than the other, nor less honorable, in proof of which the extremes of our equation have often met and exchanged places, to the great gain of themselves and of the world at large.

It is in this interconvertible feature in the industries of the world and the occasional shuffle of the actors therein that our safety lies, and which assures the advancement of civilization.

Having unloaded this sage piece of philosophy upon the reader, we will proceed to the consideration of other relevant matters. As Wellington's regiments filed out of Brussels for the fray, the Flemish women filed in with their market carts, themselves seated atop of their peas and potatoes. The British were determinedly intent on tearing a hastily erected empire down, and "Boney" and his men, further down in the woods there, were as fully set upon making their work stick! Now old Sol rose that morning broad-faced and smiling, mounted to his meridian in his usual unperturbed manner, and, like the honest body that he has ever been reputed to be, laid him down in the west, disturbed at nothing he had seen on his way

The cabbages grew as he beamed upon them, and as for the "Juke" and "Boney," he saw them tumbling over each other like pismires perturbed, but that to him was as old as cabbages, and did not excite his comment. "People might get excited about such things as that, but not the father of lights," he was heard to say, as he went to rest on his pillow of red cloud.

No more could the Brussels *frau*, for she bought her cabbage on that June morning in 1815, rightly anticipating that her household and herself would be as hungry on that day as on any other, and she put it on to boil, and as it was a Sunday dinner, she looked carefully to her broth, and when the French cavalry opened right and left like a curtain, and out of this pocket the fair lilies of the South bent wrathfully over the British squares, she tasted and said, *"Das ist gut!"*

Smooth it over as we will, Arthur Wellesley and the yellow Corsican had a genuine, old-fashioned "scrap," and disturbed the peace of the

neighborhood not a little trampled the fields of tall rye into the earth
whilst the poor frau redoubled her exertions, whacked the ball of dough
with her rolling-pin, put her sturdy arms to the work rolled the paste
flat and cut her noodles with a fierce energy not surpassed by the
fiery cuirassiers themselves. With her brow bound with bands of per-
spiration, and with many a puff and back-ache, she advanced the
courses of the feast, and as the Scots Greys swung their sabres and
advanced upon the standards of the Invincibles, upbearing the death-
less scrolls of Jena, Austerlitz, Wagram, and Friedland, she gave the
pie-tins a swirl and trimmed the edges as dexterously as the veteran of
the Old Guard sliced the liver of his foe, and as Blücher's horse fell
and rolled over him, she sprang afresh to her rolling pin and pressed
it down upon the paste with a grim pinch, as if she had a grudge against
the sturdy old Dutchman, and would finish him there and then ; and
this with some affected unction, for "Boney" had disbursed shekels
by stealth in Brussels the day before, and the Belgic mind was unde-
cided as to which side it was on '

The dear old *frau* is right. We have said it. To not many is it
given to get up a good dinner under such discouraging circumstances.
There were large promises, to be sure, and boastful. "Boney' said he
would be in Brussels to dine, and Sir Thomas Picton and the "Juke"
rode confidently, even gaily out, saying that Blücher had probably
already finished the business, and they would be back for dinner. Sir
Thomas dined not again indeed ; but had not the *schöne frau* good reason to go on with her dinner ? The guests would be there, they said ;
they were even now at the door with broken arms, and faces distraught
and powder-burnt, their boots full of blood ! And her boiling pot bub-
bled and sputtered, busily keeping time to the deep reverberations of
the guns twelve miles away. Surely the *frau* is right, for a good dinner
has done more to keep the peace than all the sermons ever preached,
however it may fail this time, and if the world were called to divide
on pot or powder, saltpetre wouldn't be in it, and the poor devils who
have each other by the ears at the bidding of " Boney " and Wellesley,
down at Mount Saint Jean, would fling away their flint-locks and fra-
ternize in a mob within the kitchen of the Belgic housewife

How many of the famishing wretches before Hougomont would
weep for joy this minute at an invitation to exchange the glory of
France for a bowl of soup'

It has been a busy day , and it is drawing to a close ; and the six o'clock dinner is not far off. "Boney," these fourteen hours, has vexedly taken up the big pinches of snuff, throwing the half away. He had a positive engagement to dine in Brussels this June Sunday, 1815, but—"He cometh not," she said!

And as the one hundred and fifty captured guns bore the insignia "Liberty," Equality, and Napoleon's cipher ("N"), so this dear old *frau* put the finishing touches on her pies by duplicating in the upper crust the hopes of the French people. And the pies and the hopes—but I can't stop to point a moral.

"Take, eat," she said, in remembrance of him who was emperor at dawn and a beggar at dusk!

Many a good man has cursed the fate that disappointed him of a hot dinner, but I can call none by name who returned from a hard day's work, and no dinner in sight, with a keener sense of his loss than the man who for twenty years had quarreled about the "jography" of Europe. The poor fellow went home in disgust, having lost his hat, his sword, his carriage, and his small change, and they put him on a crag in the midst of a drowned world—in a Soldiers' Home, mark you—fit abode of the exile, where the worms that die not, called Bitter Memory, Defeat, and Ennui, fed on his heart till he died.

And Wellesley went home also, and hung around until they stoned his house, and forced him to put iron shutters over his windows to save the glass and his life!

But there is peace and quiet these eighty years in the Flemish market gardens; the sweet sunlight falls on the blossoming peas, and the dews freshen and nourish the fringes of thyme and parsley; the children play along the hedges, and there is no death in the pot, and never was—only savory broth and sweet life!

OUR ADVERTISING DEPARTMENT.

The merchants, packers, bankers, managers of the Live Stock Exchange, manufacturers, and artists represented in this work are well-known leaders in their respective lines of business, many of them of national reputation, all of them pre eminent as successful business men, unsurpassed in public spirit and of unquestioned personal honor and commercial integrity. They are all so widely known each house so distinguished in its own peculiar field of enterprise that we feel that we are doing the economic buyer and the general public a real service by asking one and all to carefully study our advertising department. Particularly if you are a stranger and unacquainted, you will find it to your personal interest to call upon these gentlemen at their places o business, or to communicate with them through the mails.

AT THE FORT

During the summer season drill will be held in the early morning, from 7 to 8 o'clock, alternating, company drill and battalion or regimental drill.

The weekly dress parade will be held at sunset as follows Monday, 1st Battalion, 20th Infantry. Tuesday, 2d Battalion, 20th Infantry; Wednesday, Cavalry Squadrons, Thursday, Regiment of Infantry; Friday, review of the entire command.

The engineers can now be distinguished from the soldiers in other branches of the army by the change in their uniforms to dark blue trousers.

The open air concerts at the Post will be held every Monday Tuesday, and Thursday at 5 o clock.

The Home-Riverside Coal Mining Co., No. 1 Plant, Leavenworth, Kas.

THE HOME RIVERSIDE COAL MINING COMPANY, LEAVENWORTH, KANSAS

In conversation with the average citizen of Leavenworth as to her industries and possibilities as a manufacturing center, the first word that is given expression to is coal. With the thought that in all the vast expanse of country lying north of the Kaw and south of the Dakotas, west of the Missouri and east of the Rocky Mountains Leavenworth is the only coal producing county; one cannot but realize that Leavenworth, by her location, certainly is in a position to at least successfully compete with any other coal district, if not able to dictate terms. We can be brought to still closer lines when we are shown that The Home-Riverside Coal Mining Company are operating within the bounds of the city limits of that most beautiful and picturesque Missouri River city, Leavenworth, two of the largest coal producing plants in the Western country, which practically control the situation in that district.

The present volume of business being done by The Home-Riverside Coal Mining Company is only another public demonstration of what are the possibilities where good management and close attention to business are displayed.

The affairs now being handled by the above named corporation are the outgrowth of the business consolidated, arising from the producers of two of the most important coal mines in the State of Kansas, viz., "The Home" and "The Riverside", both located within the corporate limits of the city of Leavenworth.

During the year 1887 The Riverside Coal Company was formed under the management of the late James A. Bovard as president; the Riverside mine sunk and developed to successful operation

During the following year The Home Mining Company was formed under the management of Julius S. Edwards as president; the Home mine sunk and developed

The years 1887 and 1888 marked a new era in the history of the city of Leavenworth, and insured to her the distinction of becoming one of the great coal-producing centers of the West. On August 1 1894, the Riverside mine was purchased from the Kansas and Texas Coal Company by the owners of the Home mine, the two properties consolidated. This movement by the owners and management of the Home mine was considered by the citizens a display of good business judgment, and a public demonstration of confidence in the future of the city. The Home-Riverside Coal Mining Company is strictly a Kansas and Leavenworth institution; the same existing under a charter issued by virtue of the laws of the State of Kansas.

The entire capital stock of the corporation, $350,000, is held jointly by Colonel David A. McKibben, Major John M. Laing, and Hon. Harvey D. Rush, all old and respected citizens of Leavenworth.

The present management, under which the property is being successfully operated, are David A. McKibben, President; Harvey D. Rush, Vice-President; John M. Laing, Treasurer; James L. McKibben, Secretary; George W. Kierstead, Superintendent.

The personality of the management is a sufficient guarantee that the new corporation, The Home-Riverside Coal Mining Company, can be classed among the strongest in the city, both from a financial standpoint as well as ability to successfully handle the affairs of a corporation of this magnitude.

The corporation owns and controls, approximately, 4,000 acres of coal rights, besides several hundred acres of land in fee-simple and platted property within the city limits, all lying in an unbroken body. Situated approximately in the center of this vast body of coal rights, there stand the magnificent hoisting plants. The Home, No. 1, located at the corner of Second and Maple streets in Fackler's Addition; and The Riverside, No. 2, located at the east end of Santa Fé Street, in the South Side Park; both situated on the west bank of the great Missouri River; each plant with a shaft 10 feet by 14 feet by 700 feet in depth. With these shafts, which are just five thousand feet apart, are connected the underground workings of the mines, which are worked under a system known as the Longwall. These underground workings are connected by a tunnel, in size 6 feet by 6 feet by more than 6,000 feet in length, which lies directly under the bed of the Missouri River. The construction of this single piece of underground work, "the tunnel," required the combined labor, continuously, night and day, of six men for more than one year, and cost to construct more than $25,000.

"The tunnel," as it is termed, is considered one of the greatest mining engineering feats that has ever been accomplished in the West. The work was started from the face of the workings of each of the two mines, lying between which was nearly 4,000 feet of solid strata, through which the tunnel must be driven; from the point of beginning in both mines the objective point to be reached by each was the same.

On the night of December 31, 1892, the break-through was made
between the two workings, and when a sufficient opening was developed, and a line by the transit run through, it was determined that the
variation in a true line from the point of beginning in each working
was so small that it was impracticable to figure. Some of the most
expert mining engineers in the West have inspected the work and pronounced it simply wonderful

In the underground workings of these two mines more than seven
hundred feet from the surface are daily employed over seven hundred men, who dig, prepare, load, and send to the shafts, to be hoisted
to the surface, over twelve hundred tons, or 30,000 bushels, of the
black diamonds. There are employed for hauling the pit cars, in
which is loaded the coal, twenty-eight mules. After the coal is hoisted
to the surface, it is especially prepared into different grades and dis-
tributed to the trade throughout Kansas, Nebraska, and Missouri.
The coal is of the bituminous class. It is used very largely for
domestic purposes. It is also a first-class steam coal, a fact that is
appreciated by the various railroad corporations whose lines extend
through and beyond the district. For several years past there has
been annually used by the different railroad companies more than
75,000 tons.

The location of both the No. 1 and No. 2 plants is such that
either one or the other of them is reached by the tracks of all the important railway systems coming into Leavenworth. This is a great
advantage to the coal company, as they are thus enabled, without
delay, to handle their products and make quick shipments, which is
an item that is always appreciated by their patrons.

The local or city trade, which during the winter season averages
from eight to ten thousand bushels per day, is handled at The Home,
No. 1 Plant

The physical condition of the two mines both underground and
surface, is considered by those competent to judge to be equal, if not
superior, to that of any other coal property in the State A gentleman
from the East, "a coal property expert," was recently in Leavenworth
to examine these properties. After looking them over thoroughly in
every detail, he pronounced them, as to construction, equipment, general physical condition, neatness, and dispatch with which the properties were operated, the most complete and best managed that it had
ever been his experience to examine in the West While his report
was a strong one, it was conservative, and not in the least exaggerated

Since August 1st, the date of the consolidation of the two properties, there has been taken out and placed upon the market more than
two and one-half million bushels of coal, or an average of a half-mil-
lion bushels per month.   With this volume of business continued during the balance of the fiscal year, the new corporation will put upon
the market, approximately, 6,000,000 bushels per annum.   To produce
this enormous output, there are employed, directly and indirectly,
more than 800 men.   The pay-rolls amount, approximately, to $30,000
per month.

The State Prison is very like Jim Fisk's graveyard : those without
don't want to get in, and those within can't get out.   However, if you
really want to "get in," and will take the risk of getting out, you will
be admitted between the hours of one and four o'clock P. M. on Tuesday, Wednesday, and Friday.   Emmet Dalton, survivor of the Dalton
raid on the bank at Coffeyville, Kansas, is the head cutter in the tailor-
ing department.   Other "life-men" and women, and notables of long
or short terms, will be pointed out to you.